Metaphorosis

February 2018

Beautifully made speculative fiction

Also from Metaphorosis Books

Reading 5X5: Readers' Edition
Reading 5X5: Writers' Edition

Best Vegan Science Fiction & Fantasy

Best Vegan SFF of 2017
Best Vegan SFF of 2016

Metaphorosis Magazine

Metaphorosis: Best of 2017
Metaphorosis: Best of 2016
Metaphorosis 2017: The Complete stories
Metaphorosis 2016: Nearly Complete Stories
Monthly issues

by B. Morris Allen

Susurrus
Allenthology: Volume I
Tocsin: and other stories
Start with Stones: collected stories
Metaphorosis: a collection of stories

Metaphorosis

February 2018

edited by
B. Morris Allen

Metaphorosis Books

Neskowin

ISSN: 2573-136X (online)
ISBN: 978-1-64076-101-8 (e-book)
ISBN: 978-1-64076-104-9 (paperback)

February 2018

Love in Its Heart

David Z. Morris

It was the third one. The third ever, all in the same week. On the pipes, grainy handset video showed hulking masses, ungainly, asymmetrical, wobbling out of the sky. Tearing through level after level of the sprawling, towering city, girders screaming through showers of sparks. The first one on a Tuesday, a dozen commerce units over. Then another Friday, a little closer. And then on Saturday, just as the lights came on. Bang. Our zone.

It was still miles from my apartment, and I can't say I felt much fear. In a city of two billion, even the parting of twenty thousand souls seems insignificant.

Abstract. I got to the dispatch center by nine. It was in the east 370-by-fifties, perched in the fourth ring of a seven-ring office park, lit by a fairly convincing sun and circling a bedraggled courtyard garden. Better than my place, anyway.

So we all went, called out of our hovels, some still rubbing sleep out of our eyes as we loaded cleanup gear into the eight grey, sharp-angled trucks. Hoses and bins and sacks of absorbent crystals, and newly-scrubbed hazmat suits under the hard benches in the back. We were silent, not grim but indifferent, some managing troubled naps as our convoy navigated the arcing labyrinth of roads toward the crash site.

We unloaded in front of a shattered, three-story hulk. The ship had none of the sheen and polish that the movies would have you expect. It was ugly, had been ugly even before plowing through the anarchic layer-cake of a thousand thousand homes. The giant fragments left, like the cracked shell of a spent egg, were covered in wires and poles and tubes, embedded in mounds of rubble and fresh human corpses, buried and wedged and threaded and impaled. Not built for atmosphere, I could see that much — but

I left the question dangling. I wasn't paid to think, so I didn't bother.

What I did notice was the sun — the real, actual sun — emerging from a ragged tunnel torn through forty, maybe fifty stories of solid nested humanity. It seemed to dance over the corpses, giving them in death what they might have gone years without in life. It glinted from the armor of the ranks of Seattle police, and from the nearly-identical gear of the upstanding men of the U.S. Army.

The Tuesday ship had taken out plenty of ups, middles, and masses. But by Saturday the heights were empty — even my two-bit bosses were calling the shots from private bunkers at some unknown depth and distance. The corpses were people like me — too poor to hide or flee, or to have ever travelled to any edge of the city.

Still, just people — what got me was the dogs. Most were close to the surface of the pile, among the twisted remains of the higher levels. Tongues rolling out of crushed and severed heads, eyes still waiting for unworthy masters. To be rich enough to own a dog, and just leave it behind — the thought confused and saddened me.

I fought off feeling, as I fought off theories about all of this. I just bent over, picked up a metal shard and put it in one vacuum chute, or some wet, biotic chunk, and put it in the other one. Three years at Extreme Recoveries, and it almost felt like what I was made for.

Three years of sifting other people's shit and excrescence. Three years of their failed projects, lost hopes, by-products, accidents, leftovers. Like I belonged in the suit, with its empty yellow plastic slickness, a thing that never came to fit. Slogging through cisterns leaking unknown chemicals, pressure-washing breached biological facilities with hydrochloric acid, "remediating" leftover surface-to-space weapon installations.

It wasn't the life I'd hoped for, of course. Who would? I went to school for bioengineering. Life as it existed, and as it could be remade. They had been powerful, those dreams, those ambitions. But they remained vague, and quiet, and unfulfilled.

My parents were of the generation who bought into the myth of equality — born under black presidents, working under black CEOs, a brief dream in a time of plenty. They had begun to forget, begun to think that maybe we didn't have to work twice as hard. Maybe they passed that delusional ease down to me — or maybe I had just let them down. As the world became lean and hungry again, I learned how wrong they were. But not fast enough.

And with a only bachelor's degree in bioengineering, you got to clean up other people's failures.

I'm writing this now, after all that has happened, as the first and last serious product of my bioengineering research "career." It will have no audience, and little scientific value. But it soothes my soul in a time of need.

It was on that day, the third year rounding into the fourth, in the depths of my uncaring, that I reached down and saw something ... different. A smooth, chrome egg, no bigger than the palm of a hand, almost blinding in that new sun. Some sort of bomb? An alien grenade? But the army had already swept the place.

Just moments after I picked it up, the egg's gleaming surface opened with a sharp crack. Startled, I looked around, but no one was close enough to hear. It truly was an egg, with a thin shell and inside — something.

A patch of black fur, neutral and mute — but with the aura of life. I picked up the tiny chrome fragment that had fallen away. It seemed machined, unremarkable. Unthinking, I let it drop into the metal chute, which snagged it with a breathy inhalation.

I opened up my suit and my coveralls, just at the neck. I slipped the cracked egg in against my skin, felt its warmth.

In the next second, with the feeling of returning from a dream, I cursed my stupidity. Some robot going through the waste might spot that shell fragment, trace it back to me.

I kept working, picking up stray bits of cabling, the slashed veins of the data pipes. I hadn't had data in my apartment for years.

The chrome egg was still there when I walked off the site, aching, filthy despite the suit layers, back into the truck. Again, we were all silent, exhausted.

"Make a good haul today, ya black bastard?"

Except, of course, for Rollins, who had plenty of energy left to talk. I just barely lifted my gaze to meet that drawn and hungry smile, those hollowed eyes, the spiked ruff of blonde hair.

If you'd asked him, he'd tell you he was just joking, being friendly. When I'd first gotten to Extreme Recoveries, I thought I'd be gone in a few months. So I never bothered educating the man. And now I was just too tired.

"Hey Nixon, c'mon, what's up?" He kicked my boot with his — friendly.

I didn't say anything. Maybe that made me the asshole. I felt a tiny movement against my chest.

"Aw, c'mon man, don't be like that. I'm just fucking around." Even after all these years, he was still confused, maybe even really hurt, when I didn't return his ribbing with a smile. But I didn't need it. Didn't need friends at all, even if someone worthwhile had come along. As much as anything else, I was embarrassed to watch him try, in his painful, perverse way, to win me over.

I turned to catch the last disappearing wisp of natural sun. We rode on in glassy silence.

Back at base, I went into the white-plastic shower room, where I had my one moment of privacy during a ten-hour shift. I opened my shirt and reached in, and found that the shell of the egg had fallen away. I felt bits of it working deeper into the suit, sharp but pliable against my skin.

What lay revealed was black fur, a tiny nose, eyes shut tight to the world. I gently lay the tiny form, still tightly curled, on the shower's cheap plastic bench. Then, perhaps responding to my touch, four paws unfurled from the darkness, huge and searching as black yawns. I watched rapt, while carefully fishing gentle metal shards out of my suit's waistband.

Two pointed ears topped its small, sleek head. A tail twitched out, as long again as the tiny body. Like a kitten — but not quite. Too-long legs, lips that curved the wrong way around, strange, tufted antennae on the ears. I felt no threat.

I scrubbed myself without taking my eyes off of it. Its eyes stayed shut, but its thimble-sized chest rose and fell. Then I turned the water to a warm trickle, thought about it for just a moment, and lifted my charge into the flow. The creature went immediately tense in my hands, and I pulled it out the next instant. Still without opening its eyes, it flicked its head, just so, sending water droplets flying.

However persistent my scientific delusions, I can't help but include the unscientific detail of that head-flick, that single gesture.

Because that was the exact moment it was all over.

I took her home, through the maze of shuttle pods and stairwells and catwalks that bound the city's workers to the lower levels. Red light lit my steps down corridors of cold steel. Clanging boots on the walkways, the rattle of rails, delivery runners, beeping lifters, mumbled talk — the last bits of work mingling with the first bits of trouble.

We were close to the shadowed hellscape of the surface, and we all felt it. Some just schlubs like me. But plenty of predators, who saw the undercity as their safehouse, their escape route. Every time I made it into my single room without having to posture or threaten someone, I was grateful — but this time especially.

Once we were safe, I set her down. She mewled and stumbled around, her eyes still shut tight. I examined her, gently. I immediately sensed her gender, and never doubted my intuition — but there was no evidence to either support or falsify it. When I pressed the pad of one of her paws, a bristle of claws in ranked orders quilled out. I counted carefully — six toes, and hidden in each toe, twenty-eight claws, tiny and delicate. Her teeth, likewise, came in a dozen even ranks, receding back into the depths of her miniscule mouth.

I decided to name her Adesina, a name from far back in my family line. The name given to the first of my family born in America, a message to the rose-tinted future.

I didn't have much to feed her. That first night, I mixed some water and nutrient powder, offered it in a spoon, and she blindly licked at it.

As I fed her, the free pipe news chattered out of its bulletproof screen, a constant educator bolted firmly to the wall. They were talking about the descents, and you could tell that even the government talking heads were scared. Sweat snuck down the anchors' foreheads as they introduced wild speculation from suited experts. It was not just our city — these dead hulks, these uncontrollable wrecks, were hitting Jakarta, Delhi,

Osaka, Minsk, Buenos Aires. All of them unoccupied, seemingly inert. They were of no known make or model, no obvious origins. One of the experts insisted it was a Russian ploy, cooked up on Io. Another suggested Chinese. Still a third shouted wildly that they did not come from any Earth culture. Theories sparked and sputtered.

My mind drifted from the debate, and I felt no fear. I caught myself laughing mildly as I watched Adesina soak her muzzle in grainy white liquid. All any of it meant for me was warmth and fur, tentative motions, awkward steps, strange sounds from a secret mouth. Another being. A new life.

The next day, I came directly home and fed her. She blindly pawed her way around my lap. On Tuesday, my day off, I trekked to the desultory, rattling library and read a decades-old book about keeping pets. It said small mammals could drink cow's milk — a tiny cup would cost a week's check. I also used part of my data allotment to browse newer books, but they were clearly for people other than me — a single book on cat care cost more than my entire yearly salary. It wasn't until after I left that I realized I should have pulled up something on xenobiology.

On Wednesday, her eyes opened. They were large, yellow, with square pupils. Almost as soon as they opened, those eyes didn't just observe, but sought. Asked questions. Understood. She would look directly at my face, serious, serene. Her square pupils slid shut like airlock doors at each hint of brightness, so I dimmed the lights.

I thought of my own parents. They were offworld, now — able to give themselves that, at least, thank god. But no work there for me. So we talked at most once a month. They paid for the calls.

She was walking within a week — walking and more. She stalked the place, measuring and testing, pushing behind every piece of furniture. Sometimes she'd go into a tiny frenzy, ricocheting off the walls, clawing at anything soft or dangling. Twice in the first month, I came home from work, exhausted as always, to find the place a wreck, the kitchenette dismembered. Once even the fridge was open and ravaged, plastic wrap shredded, jars shattered on the floor.

Each night when I came in, I'd kneel down and scratch her between the eyes, a gesture I suppose I picked up from old movies. She would speak calmly in a strange, faerie voice. She'd rub her neck against my hand, and arch her back, and twitch her tail.

Then I made the mistake of trying to flip her over on her back and rub her belly. She exploded with rage, her ears furled and her eyes wide as her jaws gaped and her claws fanned out and down into my skin. It pricked and stung and bled, but after a brief retreat she subsided and licked my hand almost clean.

It felt familiar, earthly — but I was careful after that. I watched her with a biologist's eye, feeling old, dry knowledge unfurl within me. She grew too fast, and saw too much. Her waste came in neat, dry pellets — once a week, tiny and uniform and odorless. Within a month, she was as long as my forearm.

She resembled a creature from Earth, but was something else.

I know now how insane this sounds, how selfish and stupid. I sheltered an alien, as my world was under attack by mysterious forces. I said nothing, drew no connections, fed the alien, protected it. My curiosity had curdled years before. And what had this world ever done for me, to expect my loyalty?

I started sitting with her on the landing, in the very early hours, when we could go unnoticed. Then one day she dashed away from me. I searched for her, my gut in a knot — and a few hours later, she showed back up at the door, with a rat as big as herself in her mouth. So I started letting her in and out, at obscure hours we wordlessly agreed upon and kept to like clockwork.

She kept growing, and the ships kept falling — though less frequently. Twice, three times a month, spread out over enough of the planet that any one place began to feel almost safe again. Sometimes they even fell outside the cities, and the free pipes showed panoramas of those awful expanses — lifeless wastelands, glass deserts, glowing with industrial despoliation, crawling with diseased terrors. The greater horror our steel confinement was saving us from.

One afternoon I stood at a hamburger stall, and on a screen above the grill I saw the President. "Our naval laser cannons and detection matrix are now eliminating these threats *before* they enter the

American atmosphere. We are keeping America safe for Americans."

But I knew different. I started spending more time at the trash bars — ugly places where trashmen like me were welcome. I'd known about them for years, but never bothered. Too good for them, I'd maybe thought. But now they were invaluable. I acted like other people, sipped beers, played pool, and heard rumors. Cities were still getting hit in America. One or two a month, no matter what the free pipes and the President said. Somehow the ships were dodging the lasers, or evading detection. Or maybe the lasers didn't even exist.

I would come back from my little fact-finding expeditions, sometimes with a warm buzz, a thing I'd not allowed myself for years. And I'd lie down in my narrow, wall-mounted cot, and as I started drifting off, Adesina would pounce on my chest, with a little huffy squeak. She'd settle in, kneading those paws and their pincushion claws gently into my chest, pushing her head up against the bottom of my chin, making a slow, steady noise like the rattling of dry leaves.

Whatever she was, she loved me.

The months stretched into years. A small industry of crash-ologists sprang up, and Extreme Recoveries was acquired by a descent-consulting conglomerate. The dispatch center was moved into the bottom of a big, shining corporate campus, further up the sprawl. It was a hell of a commute, a daily pilgrimage to a more beautiful world.

There were little descent conferences there — big names on posters, all titles and prefixes. When I saw the posters, I noticed something in my chest — a hollowness, a pull. I thought, maybe in there, they're explaining all of this. And I realized that knowing mattered to me, as it hadn't in some time. Drinking coffee and listening to panel discussions didn't fit into my schedule — but the emptiness remained.

Then, two years after the first descent, with Adesina now as long as my arm, there was a chance. There was a required training on disposal unit protocol, but I knew it like the back of my hand already. And there it was, another poster — "Game Theory and the Descents." A stylized illustration of one of the falling ships. Right in the middle of the training.

So I just left Extreme Recoveries after reporting for the morning, and walked through scrubbed-clean elevated tunnels, glancing out over glowing gardens that hid the slums below. The radiating, white-lit auditorium was at the opposite edge of the campus. I sat in the back, trying not to be seen, hoping my swiveling chair wouldn't squeak.

I was the only person in coveralls. There were others in suits, and a few of that particular breed of indulged slob — the rumpled academic scientists, in wrinkled shorts and flapping buttondowns and beards. I tried to make sense of the swirls of opaquely-worded speculation.

"This is psychological," said one of the suited and slick types. "Some kind of ploy. If they actually wanted to destroy us, there would have been bombs in the ships. Fusion isn't *hard.*"

"That's not an answer!" shouted back another man on the dais. "We must assume that this is all *strategic.* I propose this thesis — there is something about the ships we have *missed.* Perhaps a virus. A slow poison. They are a preparation. A vanguard."

I thought then of Adesina. I had considered, of course, telling someone about her. She was information they could use, these big men, trying to crack the case. But I knew they would take her away from me. So I said nothing, to anyone. I began to wonder, very occasionally, if something was wrong with my mind.

But, I thought then, she didn't fit into their war-game scenarios. She wasn't a disease vector. She would never harm anyone. I'd lived in close quarters with her for two years, and I wasn't just healthy, but — I suddenly realized — happy. I would have my curiosity, but the suits and thinkers could go to hell.

Midway through the third or fourth panel, I left. I was halfway back to Extreme Recoveries when a voice rang out behind me.

"Yo, Nixon!" It was Rollins. Jesus.

He peeled towards me from a group of cleaners on their way out of the complex. They must have finished the training early. Rollins smiled broadly, his eyes bright slits over a coathanger smile. "Hey man! You over at that conference?"

I looked him flatly in the eye. Awfully lucky guess. "Yeah. I'm already certified on the new protocol, so Jorgenson said I should go to that thing instead."

"Huh," replied Rollins, rubbing the back of his head, bouncing on the balls of his feet. "Anything interesting?"

"Just a bunch of eggheads," I replied. "They don't know shit."

"The bosses, they gonna make you a scientist or something?" There it was — the aggression masking weakness. I thought of the water-lizard, a lost species which had used a delicate, expansive neck ruff to hide its tiny body.

"I don't have time to let you fuck with me, Rollins." His face collapsed in confusion as I turned to head home.

And of course, that was the day they first followed me. I noticed two men, out of the corner of my eye, like motes or shadows. You get good at that — at first I thought they were muggers. I put my hand in my pocket, making as if I were hefting something there. But they kept their distance, and I lost them.

Adesina pranced to greet me. I made my hands into playful claws and ruffled her head, then turned to the pipe. A descent in China, one outside Lagos (that happened sometimes — a near-miss). None in the U.S. of A, of course. No sir.

It wasn't until the next Sunday that they knocked on my door. I looked out of my peephole and saw them there, in dark blue jumpsuits. No insignia. More than a guy in a suit and tie, or even in body armor, you worried about those blue jumpsuits. Someone must have reported me, but no one knew.

I opened the door just a crack.

They told me my name. They said nothing about the conference, or the training I'd missed. They told me where I'd been and what I'd been doing two years before — cleaning up Descent Number Three.

Then they stopped telling, and started asking. I told them yes, I'd been on that site, but no, I didn't remember tagging or chuting anything unusual, no. They asked if they could come in, and I told them, no, I'm really sorry, but I've got a guest in here, and I made with some eye-bugging and an uncomfortable laugh and a sleepy lascivious grin. It would have made my grandfather roll over in his grave twice — he was the Attorney General of Nevada.

They looked at each other, and I saw them thinking just what I wanted them to — these lower-level boys, they got nothing on their minds but pussy. One of them shrugged and tapped something on his wrist, and they left. Of course, the truth was I hadn't had a girl around in years, but getting those jumpsuits off my doorstep felt better than any lay I could remember.

When I closed the crack of the door and turned around, though, Adesina had her back up against the far wall, her entire body arched and tense, her claws out in their terrifying ranks, her eyes glowing gold so bright it was almost blinding. Just as I shut the door to the outside world, her mouth opened and I saw her hundreds of razor-shard teeth, and a sound came out like the shattering of a tiny planet. It pushed me back against the door, knocked cans from a shelf.

Something changed after that. Snoop-theories started flowing through the trash bars — the jumpsuits were asking everybody questions, all the crews, and they all had their own ideas about why. For me it was a relief — they weren't targeting me. They didn't know about my Adesina.

But she started growing again. She'd still lie on my chest, her eyes closed as I stroked her. But within weeks of that unwelcome visit, her head tucked right under my chin and she stretched all the way down over my hips. By then she weighed nearly forty pounds. I got short of breath with her on top of me, and so I started pushing her off, leaving her to squeeze narrowly onto one side of the cot. She got used to it, I guess.

Things were even trickier when we played. One day I ruffled her ears, and she swatted at me, and I swatted back, and in the next second I noticed that the flesh between my thumb and forefinger was open like a wet mouth, a steady trickle of blood dropping to the floor. She hadn't even tried to hurt me.

I was used to no one giving a damn about me, so I didn't think twice about showing up to work with a bandaged hand. But Rollins noticed. I saw him stare at it — but he didn't say anything. He had gotten quieter, and I started seeing something in his eyes beyond half-friendly stupidity. Something inquiring.

Men started following me home more regularly. I stopped letting Adesina out. She turned moody, would spend hours curled up in a corner, alone, uninterested in me, one sleeping eye open. But she kept growing, and started eating so much I had to feed her cheap cultured food — the sort of flavorless pseudo-protein paste the Light Church fed to indigents. She didn't seem to care. Just kept staring at the door.

Then one night, she leapt up to join me on the cot — and the wall creaked. She halfheartedly tried to find a place to lay, but there was nowhere for her. I looked at her standing above me, searching, confused, and saw her as if I'd never seen her before.

The tiny thing I'd pulled out of a metal egg was now a hundred or a hundred and twenty pounds. Five feet long from nose to tail. And beneath that black coat I still thought of as warm and comforting — muscle, as hard as my own. Without leaving the room, without good food, she had grown into a creature of the jungle. Of another world's jungle.

That night, she slept on the floor. I made a nest for her out of blankets. But we couldn't stay. The net was closing.

I thought about it for days, on my way to and from Extreme Recoveries, watching over my shoulder, in and out of the dark hole I called home. The free pipes regularly streamed their panoramas of the desolate and unlivable land beyond the city. But there were different stories in the streets, in the trash bars. I'd heard them from my family, too, as a kid — tales of places beyond the city, where people could go. Some said they even knew people who had gone — people who were never heard from again. Nothing more than vague whispers passed among the cities' dreaming miscreants. A talisman of hope, like an unscratched lottery ticket.

It wasn't a good option.

I packed up a few things, put on a long coat. We left in the latest part of night, climbed down stairways that became more and more rickety, jumped across jagged walkway gaps, until I was finally climbing hand over hand down masses of rebar, tangled through skeletal steel frames that cut and ripped and shuddered with my weight.

I worried at first what Adesina would make of this place, how she would behave, whether she would even stay with me — but she followed without hesitation or confusion. Where I panted and teetered and hurled my body like a wobbling football, she gracefully arced through the darkness, flowed with light feet down impossible rails, dropped with cold certainty into one black pit after another, and waited for me, unscathed, at the bottom.

We were alone for a time, but as we went deeper, we began to see others. These were the scarred and twisted denizens of the lowest places, unwanted by anyone or anyplace else, even in the vastness of the city. There were lean-tos of blue tarpaulin, wrapped tight into hovels and wedged against pilings. Under them sat men with no noses, no eyes, no hands. We saw huddled clutches of children, naked and squalling like puppies at their dying mothers' dry teats.

And of course, there were the other kinds of outcasts — the toughs who banded together here, out of sight of the authorities. We glimpsed neon now and again, heard voices raised in brittle revelry. The welcome warning of danger.

But we couldn't avoid all trouble. From above, I'd spotted a rope bridge, a delicate pathway over a seemingly bottomless chasm — and at its head, a massive, hooded figure, holding a spiked iron club in one meaty, deformed hand. I scouted for ways around, but there was no other path.

So I approached him, and was relieved when Adesina seemed to disappear. I held myself straight, my arms at my side, unsure even of how to look menacing.

"There's a toll here," said the hulking man, a not-quite-human voice emerging from the darkness of the hood. But before I could reply, Adesina emerged beside me, her shoulder now as high as my elbow.

The tollman regarded her coolly for a moment, in shock or indifference. Then she stepped forward mildly, dropping her head as her jaw unfurled, and loosed that planet-splitting hurricane of a roar.

The brutish tollman tumbled back, his club ricocheting into the chasm as he scrambled to keep his balance. Then he turned and fled across the bridge, into the shadows. We didn't see him again.

And then finally, finally we reached it — the muck on which the city floated, the end of our descent. The light here was red and thin, like sickly blood. There was dirt — not the groomed dirt of an elevated garden, with its fluffy clumps that rolled out of your hand. This was dead earth, sticky, frozen in glutinous waves, full of bits of garbage fallen from higher levels; iron bars and rusted car parts and split batteries spilling acid; glowing slicks of strange lace over every diseased surface.

Great lichen grew on the carcasses of ancient traincars. Tremendous, pale-eyed rodents gnawed at tangles of rust — and fled at Adesina's scent. Every twenty yards stood the mass girders, so often hidden on the higher levels. Like steel tree trunks, forty feet around, spattered with filth and hard-earned graffiti — the foundations of the world.

This, certainly, looked like the outside world shown on the free pipes — nothing but mud and the skeletons of a dead past. Still, we were lucky. It was January, cool and dry. Three months later, the place became a floodcatch for the summer.

Adesina moved through it all with such smooth and untroubled confidence that I couldn't shake the suspicion that she had been there before, somehow — that she had gone far beyond the boundaries of the neighborhood on those early morning wanderings, that she had dreamed her way here as she lay entombed in my bedsit.

But still, she was alert, orbiting me like a nervous moon, flitting from one shadow to the next, disappearing and reappearing as I moved in the vague direction of a half-heard memory.

Any threats were gone before I knew. More than once, I felt the air go tense, heard an abbreviated grunt or hiss, and waited as she slunk back to my side, breathing heavily, her jaws dripping.

We moved for days, barely stopping to rest. There was no change in the light — not even the half-imagined traces of sun I treasured at high noon on a low city Saturday. I had only ever moved through the city on lifts and trams and winding walkways, and had no sense of when we might reach its edge. After ten days, I was out of food. After two weeks, when she brought me the corpses of sick and diseased and horrible creatures, I shared them with her, gratefully.

On the fifteenth day, or the twentieth, we rounded a corner — I in front, and Adesina roaming loosely at my heels — and there was a huge black shape there, and something flashed white in it, and I felt a violent blast to my chest. There were sharp pinpricks as I fell back, then rending pain — and then came another blunt impact, lifting the weight from me.

I scrambled to my knees, and saw Adesina grappling, hissing, clawing with a ferocity I'd never dreamed of — tangled with another creature that looked exactly like her.

In the next second, another figure emerged, running — a woman with red hair, matted and tangled, her round, defeated face contorted in panic and sadness as she ran towards the enraged pair of beasts.

"Stop, stop!" she cried, and she threw herself into the fray, and somehow she wrapped one of them in a bear hug (I could not tell them apart) and separated them bodily, even as claws and spittle flew around her.

She lay there, panting, not half as big as the creature she gripped. It roared and twisted and flailed, but the woman did not let go, though a flap of her face lay open like a curtain, streaming blood.

I stood, stunned, my mind reeling. The other creature backed nervously towards me, away from the entwined pair, and I thought it must be Adesina. I put my hand on her head, gently, and she calmed. I saw she was missing tufts of hair.

Then the other two slowed, untangled, and turned to face us. We all panted.

I looked at Adesina, and at the other creature. This was not how animals worked. Not how life worked. Variation was the heart of any natural species — different tones, eyes, shapes, angles. But these two were not simply of the same kind — they were truly identical. The same size, precisely. Their ears tufted in the same strange way, twitching with the same tension. Their eyes were the same shape and size. They were indistinguishable — except that Adesina now hugged close to my side.

"What ... what is this?" It was all I could manage.

The woman ignored her mauled face, staring numbly at the ground, not meeting my confused eyes. Her clothes were ragged and torn, and stained with blood all over. I thought of my hand, still carrying its accidental scar.

"You haven't seen others, then," she said, not a question, but an inflection of disconnected madness echoing sorrow into the space between us. "They are Drexal," she continued. "They are heralds. Bait. Traps."

Her hand rested on the other creature's head, and absently scratched between its eyes. It stared at Adesina, and Adesina stared back.

"Did you find an egg?" I dared to ask.

"It found me," she said, her lips moist and loose. "They found us." Then I saw the tag on her wrist — a medical designation of some sort, condemning its wearer to one of the towers for the sick or disturbed. The woman was on the verge of tears. "She made me happy, damn her."

And with that, she backed away, eyes darting. The great beast backed after her, its head low and haunches tense, its eyes not leaving us until it had disappeared into the bloody shadows.

We travelled for many more days after that. I became wasted and sick with bad food and poisonous water. But finally, a thing began to happen that I could hardly fathom — the city began to fade above us. When I looked up, I could distinguish the shadow of one looming tower from the next. During the day, true light began to reach us, first in a putrid yellow wash — and then, one day, there was a dusty, golden sunbeam, and I stood and let it warm my face for three hours.

There were scraps of grass, then plants, and then, as if in a dream, we were *outside*. And it was nothing like the pipes showed. It was like a platform garden that went on and on. The wind was an animal, playing against my face. In the distance, during the daytime, I saw the earth rising to meet the sky, covered in more green than I had ever seen, but also brown, and far away, farther away than my eyes had ever reached before, beautiful rising angles of grey and blue and white.

Adesina was unnerved. She twitched at every waving blade of grass, ripped bushes from their roots when they brushed her flanks, pawed at pools of water and hissed at her own image. But before long, she once again wandered far afield, and hunted, and brought me a new kind of prey — rabbits and birds, things out of books, more and better food than I had ever known. I knew that we were supposed to cook them, but I had no clue how — and they were still delicious.

I regained my strength, and then some. With Adesina curled beside me, I slept in beds of grass, and dreamed shapeless, vertiginous dreams. The world inside my head expanded to fill the world outside.

Then I thought of something, and for the first time looked back at the city. It was a massive aberration, smoking, flashing. It revolted me — but day by day it shrank behind us, until it was no bigger than the distant mountains.

I thought about the woman, and what she'd said. Adesina, and the other one like her — the woman had called them Drexal. They had found us. She'd been a madwoman. Yet she had pushed me closer to a certain dark knowledge. But now more than ever, I needed my strange companion, and I evaded that knowledge fiercely — just as I now saw, for the first time in the flesh, rabbits and grouse frantically evading eagles.

After leaving the shadow of the city, Adesina had grown again, now to six or seven feet long. We moved easily over the rolling, open land, unconcerned for many days about anything but the ground beneath our feet, and where the whispered promised land might show itself. But then, one morning, there was a low whirring in the air — a mechanical sound that drew me jarringly back to the city. I hissed at Adesina, who disappeared, and hid myself behind a rocky outcropping.

It was a large delivery drone, hefting a man-sized crate beneath its rotors. I watched its path, and when it was gone, we moved cautiously to follow it, keeping a lower profile. We spotted two more craft in the next few days, one some kind of menacing scanner luckily spotted from afar — but one a passenger vehicle, a large clear bubble showing the profile of dozens of people. It was hard to be sure, but I caught an impression of leisure from within that bubble.

It was not long before we came upon its destination. In a valley, a wandering row of boxes spread along a river and up an embankment — buildings, the kind that were common before the cities rose. From a faraway perch, I saw opulent silver statues and expansive gardens, carefully sculpted paths, playing fields and geometric pools of water. More drones came and went, in many directions, as tiny human shapes moved among it all. And, intermittently, a menacing laser would scan the surroundings, or a martial robot fly or roll into sight. We retreated before we could be spotted, taking a wide circle around the place.

This, I realized, was what the ups were hiding, why the free pipes insisted that the world outside the city was poison. I imagined dozens of opulent settlements like this, escapes from the city and its rabble. We kept the engines pumping for them, ran the hydroponic farms and the toothbrush factories, programmed the drones and crafted vapid distractions for the premium pipes. We stayed out of the way, confining our trouble to the lower levels of pocket worlds, while they wandered the unspoiled earth. I hoped that these were not the Edens that had been whispered of, for my soul knew they would execute me on sight.

So we moved on and on, and my clothes had nearly fallen away by the time we saw the first people. They appeared far in the distance, on a green expanse, and I felt Adesina hide herself. Over the next day, I spotted them again and again, moving closer, and I walked towards them, Adesina trailing invisibly behind. Finally, we met, and they approached me openly, easily and calmly — a group of four men. They carried long spears, and the tallest among them held a primitive gun. Their hair was matted and wild, their skin darkened by the sun, and they wore beards — all now true of me, as well.

When they were thirty feet away, they stopped, and then I stopped. There was something joyous about their manner, nothing of threat or anxiety.

"Hello," the tallest one said. "Do you mean us harm?"

"None," I replied. And I held out my naked palms.

"Then welcome."

The village was crude, but beautiful — buildings of wood and stone, touching the earth, full of children. It was surrounded by lush farmland, and I adapted quickly to tending the plants, mending tools, digging trenches to carry water from streams and wells into the rows. Some of the people had childhood memories of the city, but most had been born in this place. They listened to my descriptions of life in that tangle of metal and electricity with rapt horror.

Adesina disappeared after I went with the men — but I knew she hadn't gone far. A week after I arrived, as I tentatively explored the forest near the village, she quietly emerged from the shadow of a massive tree to meet me. She was larger still, now — her shoulders as high as mine, her body ten feet long, her ear-tufts brushing the lower branches. But she lowered her head, and I rubbed between her eyes, and she butted me in the chest playfully. Then she sat, looking down on me, her eyes more gentle and sad than I had ever seen.

We continued to meet there, in the woods, but she never showed herself to the villagers, and I never spoke of her. So we lived separately for those months, and I imagined her joyful life in the wild as I reveled in the warmth of the village. Extreme Recoveries, the falling ships, Rollins and all he stood for, seemed like distant things. Nothing but stories. I spent my nights welcomed in the modest huts of my new family, nestling into my new life.

I had been the first arrival from the city in half a generation — but suddenly, more began to come. First two, then five, then ten. The village took them in as they had me, and like me, they rejoiced in the place, and there was no strife.

But these new arrivals also shared stories explaining their exodus, huddled around fires like the primitives of the deep past.

"All the same. No motive, no suspect, just piles of gore, heads severed. High up or low down, doesn't matter a bit," said an old woman, a miracle she'd made it out.

"They found my son, in the play yard, he was ..." The young mother couldn't finish.

"I walked into the garden, he had just been out to tend the tomatoes. He loved a fresh tomato." I loathed the widowed heiress, even as I pitied her.

Blood dried into ribbons across the streets, unnumbered thousands cut down.

"Even on the elite pipes, we pay good money for information, and they gave us nothing — NOTHING." The businessman, in the soiled remnants of the suit he had worn in his rush to flee, was indignant and terrified. "Dark shapes, they say. Huge but unseen. The ramblings of a bunch of lower-level drunks," he huffed. Then, remembering himself, he apologized with his wounded eyes.

I wondered if his world was more shattered than mine.

"It isn't the murders," said a preternaturally calm young man, the fire glinting against his cracked spectacles. "A thousand deaths, ten thousand — who would notice? The problem is the unknown. The paranoia. Panic is starting to set in. Streetcorner doomsayers. New cults, dark prophecies. Hate groups,

blaming the gays, blaming the blacks ...”
And he trailed off, looking at me, as if this
would surprise me in the least.

Again my mind dredged up the sick
woman, with her madness and her
medical tag, and Adesina’s furious twin.
Yet I refused to understand. I see that
now, and I blame myself — but what
could I have done?

So I continued to farm, began to think
of the rest of my life out there in beauty,
let the city and its problems devolve to
someone else. I built a hut of my own, a
crude thing of mud and thatch, at the
edge of the woods.

Still Adesina came to me when I went
into the trees, and lowered her head, and
sometimes we even wrestled, and she was
gentle and joyful. She seemed to sense
when I was alone in my hut, and some
nights she wriggled through the door, and
lay next to me as we once had — but now
she cradled me on her rising and falling
chest. I had never slept so well.

Then the final new arrival came. He
stumbled across the grasslands, just as
all the others had — and I carried a spear
as we went to meet him. He looked at me,
and looked at the others with me, and I
saw in his wide eyes wonder, fear,

disbelief, suspicion, hope. It was Rollins, the edges of his face softer, the angle of his body opened. I felt a tiny curl of the past rise in my chest, but said nothing as we took him back. All that was over now.

He also said nothing, did not nod or wink or smile. He only spoke of the city, lost, toppled, burning. It was not the descents, no — the cults had risen, fear had taken hold, chaos reigned. Refugees had fled in every direction, he said, more bloodshed as the remnants of the police and army tried to stop them, penning them in the cities 'for their own protection.' When we retired that night, I was worried no more or less than the rest of the villagers.

The next morning, he was at the door of my hut, polite and still. I didn't let him in, because Adesina was inside, breathing deeply, curled against the length of two walls. But we sat in the grass, and he asked me about my life here. I told him I was happier than I had ever been, and the sadness that washed over him, the sudden tenderness of him, surprised me.

But suddenly the past came back to me, in the form of paranoia. "How ... how did you come *here*? Of all the directions to flee, how did you choose this one?"

"Oh, you know," he said, "Just street rumors." He gave a forced laugh, and something flared red within me.

"I have to ask you something, too." He plucked at the grass with a wonder only barely overshadowed by some other darkness.

"Go ahead," I replied, old caution suddenly remembered.

"You found one, didn't you? One of the eggs."

He watched my face. After years of control, of yes sirs, of the mask — in that moment, when I needed it most, my face betrayed me.

He looked back down. "I'm sorry we couldn't be friends, Nixon. I tried. But I tried wrong, I know that now." He paused for another moment, looking up at the clear morning sun.

"I really hoped we could be friends. But they didn't give me any choice."

And then I saw them — a dozen men in blue jumpsuits, carrying heavy packs, hefting black guns, flanked by robots crawling on six legs. They appeared over a gentle rise, as if from nowhere.

Rollins stood. From somewhere, he pulled a pistol and trained it on me. His hand shook.

"They told me you have one of the ... the creatures that's doing this," said Rollins, his eyes weirdly distant, his voice taut and fearful. "They have to be stopped. You left before they made their move — you're a sharp one, I always knew that."

Two soldiers seized me from behind, and two others advanced on my hut, hunched as turtles, large guns held before them like holy relics.

My knees were weak. "Rollins ... Rollins, what have you done?" Of course, I knew the answer. But I had nothing else to say.

Adesina rocketed from the door of the hut, and there was only one tiny, pitiful pop before the advancing men lay dead, obscenely mauled. The soldiers holding me dropped my arms and scrambled for weapons.

She moved like water, like smoke. She crushed one of their heads in her jaws, the metal of his helmet plinking with a hundred diamond punctures. I heard a horrendous sound, like a wet mattress tearing, and felt a spray. I looked, and saw Rollins holding his spewing guts as if cradling a baby. Adesina flowed sinuously towards the woods.

As Rollins lay down to bleed to death, I saw more shapes moving in the woods — and in the village. The soldiers raised their guns, trained them on my daughter, my love — and the villagers rushed the soldiers. In moments, dozens lay dead or dying. But I saw Adesina's shadow move smoothly into the trees.

Rollins was whispering something through bubbling blood. "There are hundreds of them ... thousands." He coughed and shuddered. "Help. Find them. Save us." And then he died.

Then came the firestorm. Over the next few days I saw more and more of Adesina's kin, if that was the right word. Black monsters, roaming freely now — all of them identically long and clawed and tufted. Impossibly identical. Such uniformity could not even be engineered, by any means I'd ever heard of. The environment had too much impact on a growing creature; even clones wound up slightly different.

But not these. Identical in form, and in function. Fighting the soldiers, fighting the villagers — though fighting wasn't the right word. Killing everything. The robots, the armor, the machine guns were useless.

Then came thundering choppers, hovering as they spewed lasers at the Drexal — but again and again, I saw the great beasts unleash their unnatural roars into the sky, saw the craft judder and slide to the ground.

Then came the jets and bombers, and when each missile or explosive whistled its descent, their targets fled into the trees faster than the wind, leaving the bombs to destroy only the land, to kill more and more of the survivors.

In all of this, some of the creatures were harmed — but not many.

I watched as the battle decimated the village, and watched the flashes of other battles, across the plains, on the flanks of the distant mountains. I knew I could do nothing to save my new family. Even the ups, in their mountainside playgrounds, would barely outlast the cities. But Adesina endured, appearing, covered in gore and radiating violence, to stop every threat that neared my hut.

Her protectiveness remained — but her affection was gone. And that is the truth of the Drexal. They found us in our deepest need — a need that was everywhere. They found homes, they found love — real love, I still choose to believe. The Drexal (I will never know where the name came from, whether the ramblings of a madwoman, or some secret singular connection to its source) did not know what plan they were a part of. Their lives, for them, were not stratagems or affectations — they loved, and were loved, in the way they had been made. This, I still choose to believe.

But the Drexal's love was destined to take on the enraged and defensive character of our own selfish regard. To feed terror with passion. When the time came, they showed their love in the way our world had taught them. They settled scores. They cleared ledgers. They protected — with a determination that was final.

This was how they were made. And how we made them.

So I sit to write this, as death mounts ever higher. I sit, and I wait, in this village, desolated like villages and hovels and secret resorts and burning cities across a world bigger and more beautiful than I had ever imagined.

I am alone now, save for Adesina. All I see of the final few beloved are the Drexal that roam on their behalf. They rage against each other, too — though always to a stalemate. Adesina comes back to me wounded, slinking, and with the last of each day's strength she fetches some new corpse — beasts, men, women, children. Unloved. I cannot scold her, I cannot stop her — she is fifteen feet long, and must weigh nearly five thousand pounds.

And I am hungry beyond reason, so with a heart full of horror, I eat what she brings me, and nestle in her blood-drenched fur.

I wait eagerly for those who gave us these gifts. Not because I long for an end — but because I long to know the shape of what we've invited.

What will the ships be like? The real ships — not the shattered eggs that ferried the hidden Drexal to the surface, but the chariots of their masters? Will they glitter fearsomely, as they descend onto this forsaken planet? Will they be black and unreflecting? Will they open to reveal something with limbs, and heads, and eyes? Or will there be something more terrible, something shapeless, or spaceless — something unlovable, twisting out of lost dimensions to take its prize?

Will we even know them when they come? Perhaps they are already here.

Perhaps they are nothing but the return of this darkness to my heart.

Adesina, my dearest, our love has burned a path.

Let the bastards have what's left.

About the story

This story was inspired directly by a real cat named Nebula. My wife badly wanted a cat, but this one was practically demonic - the incidents of accidental mutilation in the story, but also the sense of deep attachment to something dangerous - came from Nebula. She disappeared when we briefly left a window open on a hot Tampa night.

The story's themes of race, exploitation, and alienation are lifelong concerns of mine. I grew up partly in Japan in the early '90s, where being a white person made me stand out dramatically. That's a very different matter than being black in the United States, since it comes with at least as much privilege as alienation. But I was followed suspiciously around toy stores as a child, and strangers often wanted to touch my and my brothers' hair. It wasn't oppression, but it was deeply and permanently unnerving.

I've since devoted most of my life to understanding how people treat those they see as different. This story was first drafted in 2014, but even then I was skeptical of the idea that America was moving past its founding racial crimes. I'm saddened, but not surprised, that the cycle of history has made this story more obviously relevant now than it was when I started working on it.

The writing of the story was one of those moments you treasure - it all essentially came out at once, even at a time when I was under a huge amount of stress. I'd just left my career as an academic researcher to write full-time, and was patching together a living with freelance gigs and commercial copywriting. I've come a long way since then, but I think the story reflects the real economic anxiety I was feeling at the time, and which, frankly, most people in the U.S. and around the world now live with permanently.

So obviously, it's a dark story, with some dark predictions - but I want to be clear that I'm not an advocate of nihilism in any form. Despite our many anxieties, we still live in the most prosperous time in human history, and in many ways the most just. We can't give in to bitterness over the ways our world still isn't perfect, or abandon hope when we see what look like impossible problems. We will absolutely assure our destruction if we refuse to see it coming - but acknowledging our failures is not the same as accepting them as inevitable.

A question for the author

Q: If you could have a meal with a character from any classic novel, whom would you choose?

A: It would be Samuel Beckett's Watt. We would share a single bean, thinly sliced.

About the author

David Z. Morris is a fiction writer, journalist, and social scientist. He lived in Fort Worth, Nagoya, Austin, Tokyo, and Tampa before making it to New York City. He is married to the painter Georgia Hourdas and holds a PhD from the University of Iowa.

www.davidzmorris.com, @davidzmorris

Cheminagium

David Gallay

Pain, true pain, lives outside of time. It arrives in a shear of liminal precognition, the thudding sky before the storm. We formulate routes of escape, believing that the visitor darkening our door could be turned away with the right words. It doesn't matter what we do, what we say, whether the heart is flooded by prayers or screams.

Pain is patient.

The door always opens.

Col is only an arm's length away, huddled in his bed, a naked foot dangling over an empty boot, but I can't hear him. The ringing migraine swallows every word he says.

I press my thumbs to my ears and shake my head until my jaw clicks.

" ... worse today?"

"I'm fine."

I make my way over to the window and rest my forehead on the cold glass. Outside, the first wisps of snow kick through the leaves. My eyes drift up from a patch of wildflowers sheltering in the lee of the woodpile, over the dawn-gilt crowns of linden, towards the towering heart of Spire Iberos. I squint into the glazed eyes of the keep. Usually they are dead as a fish, but this morning, there is movement. A candle floats from room to room like a stray thought.

"Our guest appears to have settled in," Col says. "He stopped by last night, while you were out. Nothing like the shaggy weed I remember. Barely recognized him. Twice, I mistook him for Mislav and had to bite my tongue. Remember that one, our bald cousin?"

Of course, I do. Mislav was once a frequent visitor to Iberos, related to us by some stray weave of marriage. His head gleamed like sea-glass. We used to wonder if he shaved it every morning or if that was simply his skull, painted and polished. He vanished out on the Ore-Fist curs a long time back.

In the keep, the candle flickers out.

"If you're looking for an excuse," Col says, "the mules he rode in on have been rooting up and down the hill, careless for next season's crop. Remind him where the stables are, make sure the bolts aren't rusted."

"Eir or Adal can take care of it."

A flash of annoyance crosses his face. He's always been ambivalent to our huldufólk, giving their ancient, withered bodies no more thought than one would a chair or broom.

"They have their own responsibilities," he sighs. "And you need a breath of light. Go see him."

There's nothing more he'd like than to shove me out the door, into the snow. But he can barely stand. Although we are brothers in decrepitude, his ruin exceeds my own. Instead, he rolls back to his patchwork map of Casses, our domain, our country, an island beset on all compass points by unpassable seas. The

map is scored with pale chalk lines, one
for each mystic curs seared into the
landscape. These invisible rivers of velti
old-magic radiate from the wellsprings of
the Blessed: Spire Centonica at the tip of
the southern archipelago, Spire Palus
deep in the wild cliffs, and our home,
Spire Iberos, an old iron nail struck into
the toes of the northern mountains.
Practiced travelers like Col can ride the
curses from coast to coast without
missing a meal. Used to be he'd be gone
for weeks cataloguing those liminal
pathways. Wearing his chalks down to the
nub. Whenever I assumed the worst, that
he'd finally lost himself to the blur of
obsession, I'd inevitably find him curled
up in bed, snoring that same musical
wheeze from the days we shared a twin's
crib, when his lungs were clean and his
linens free of red.

The swallowing chain. A fish you cannot
see. Yearning for the unlit taper. To crawl
beneath your own spine. A long visit from
a bad friend. Sleeping in the nailed bed.
An argument with birth. The Blessed have
a thousand words to describe suffering

and just as many reasons given for it to exist. Pain is the cost of vigilance, for we Blessed stand watch on the bridge between Casses and darker countries beyond the sea, under the hills. Others believe that pain is a burden, a punishment, passed down from mark to mark, throat to throat. A reminder that the velti was never meant for us.

I learned most of this from my mother. As she tapped drops of poppy milk onto her lips, I asked how it was possible her Blessing brought her so much misery. After all, she could swim through the air as easily as an otter through the water. How could that be anything but joyful?

She gazed out the window. Her jaw already trembled from the bone-fever.

I yearn to touch the sun, she said. *I would give up everything. The desire consumes every spare thought. I dream of plunging my head into its fire, letting it consume me. I've flown so high that I could see over the mountains, to the sea. I would have gone further if my body let me, if my waking mind didn't froth into oblivion. Judoc, my darling, I would stab you in the heart right now if it offered even the slightest chance.*

Col was right about the mules. One has already breached the neighboring meadow, its flanks thick with burrs, while the other nearly snapped a leg by lodging its hoof down a rabbit burrow. With a calm but firm hand, I prod them uphill to the stalls. While drawing up a bucket from a well rimed with ice, I become aware of a figure crouched on the hill. He has a feral aspect, like a crow eying the seed in your palm.

"I had forgotten all about the mules," he says. "Seems I'm a bit fog-brained today."

"No worries. The curses can suck the wind from you."

Stig stands and approaches. He seems taller than I remember, or perhaps just thinner, stretched out. A worn cloak drapes off his lanky shoulders like moss from an alder. At the last moment he remembers to raise his chin up for a formal greeting. The mark on his throat is a scorch in the sand, mirrored glyphs of fortune. I desperately want to touch it. Instead, I mirror his posture so that he can acknowledge my own mark.

"My dearest, my Judoc. What brings that look of disbelief? Is it this?" he asks, rubbing his scalp. "Or this?" He taps his mark.

"That you're here at all."

"When I heard about Col –"

"Is that the nature of your Blessing? To hear the death clarion from the far side of Casses? Or perhaps you came to spark the kindling on his funeral pyre?"

The stinging words fly faster than I can swallow them back down. Stig accepts each blow.

"That would be something, wouldn't it? No, my gift deals with the flow of reason. Watch ..."

He bends down and plucks a dead leaf off the ground. He makes a fist and crushes it inside, close to my face so that I can hear the dry crackling of its destruction. A pattern of greenish burn scars scores his knuckles and wrists, in some places carved down to the bone.

When he opens his hand, there are only flakes of copper.

"What do you see?" he asks.

"Nothing," I say, cautiously. "Dust."

"Then we agree, it was once one thing and now is another. What compelled that transformation?"

"You did. With your hands."

I sense a child's trick, such as when Col juggles acorns and they vanish in midair, only to reappear days later in my boots. Velti magic runs through the veins of the Blessed like a translucent thread. Col's acorns, the suck of breath when my mother's feet lifted from the ground, every curs weaving its way across the earth, the hum of rooted bones and witch-ravens weeping in the cliffs. I have my own meager gifts, and it appears Stig has found his as well, although I'm at a loss how. The mark is a birthright of the Blessed. It can neither be earned nor forged.

"Before the movement, before the thought, there was the intention. An intention birthed by your presence."

The migraine, absent until now, begins to make itself known again.

"You're saying I crushed the leaf."

"That's one way of putting it. I could also blame the mules, at which point I would have to blame myself, and then so on, and so forth. We can follow the water upstream and never reach the source."

"Then what does it matter?"

"Let's say I returned home a season ago?" He takes my hand, sweeps the remains of the leaf into my palm.

Before I can answer, he covers my hands with his own.

He closes his eyes. Fog drifts from his lips.

When it is over, I am holding neither dust nor the dead leaf reconstituted.

It is a honeybee, shivering in the wind. I protectively cup my fingers around it.

"The sun is peaking," he says and there's that half-smile I remember, those exquisite angles hiding under the softness of age. "Best get on with the day. I do promise to keep more watchful eye on the mules."

"Right. There's should be some chestnuts in the storehouse that haven't moldered yet. Keep them away from the western slope, there's a line of belladonna that'll turn them into frothing bags. If you want, I can send up a hulda to help. You remember Adal, don't you? He still has a touch with animals."

"No. Your huldufólk won't be necessary."

As I make my way down the hill, he calls after me.

"I searched for you last night, up in the keep, but the other chambers were all bolted or destitute. If my arrival has brought you any discomfort – "

A tingling pain flares in the crease of my palm. Stinger torn away, the bee curls up and dies. I scuff a hole in the dirt with my heel and gently place it inside.

"I forgot, you weren't here," I answer without turning around. "The bone fever consumed our parents, one after the other. That was a long time ago. Me and Col ... we sleep in the common halls now. The keep belongs to the spiders."

The last time Stig and I spoke, adolescence still dripped from our noses. We were deep in the trenches of another Iberos winter. Despite the freezing bite of the clearing sky, the walls of the kitchens were already sweating. Stig stood at the cutting board, thin as a reed, hunched over a platter of smoked eel. Focused on the sweep of the butcher's blade, he noted my approach with a sarcastic bob of deference.

I didn't expect to see you, divine one, he said between decapitations. *Rumor was you'd taken to your blankets again.*

Most unmarked wouldn't dare speak to a Blessed with such brazenness; it was only our friendship that granted him protection. As my own parents were often preoccupied and Col had grown bored with entertaining his smaller brother, most of my childhood lingered with Stig and his clan. His uncle especially treated us both like sons. We sat at his feet as he worked the potter's wheel and regaled us with stories of his people, gods and queens, pirates and demons. Me and Col spent a hundred afternoons staring at the treasures paraded across the shelves of his uncle's shop, ancient relics to be revered but never touched. Whenever our friendship bore injuries over the jagged shoals of boyhood, his uncle reminded us that good men are strengthened by their scars.

Col must have already been through here, I said. *No doubt spreading rumors of my condition while picking bones from his own teeth.*

Not my place to say, Stig laughed. *Fact is you look rotted. Let's take care of that.*

With three knocks on the wall, Maeija appeared out of the gloom. Like most huldufólk, she was a shrunken, pitiful creature, swathed in linens that barely disguised her oaken complexion and the weeping wounds of blue gaslight. While Spire Iberos may have had many tenants over its life, lore had Maeija a constant fixture, serving drinks and scrubbing floors back to the primordial mud. I would not be surprised if she was there to greet the first Blessed when they descended onto Casses in a storm of falling stars.

Of course, Maeija never bowed to me. A hulda has no need to acknowledge its rung on the ladder. With the buzz of cicadas under her breath, she addressed me in their strange backwards language, where tomorrow has already happened and yesterday is yet to come.

My Blessed, I recalled this threshing in your skull. If I served you better, would the pain have fled more swiftly?

Without another word, she slipped away and returned with an ivory cup. Her tea smelled foul, with bits of unidentifiable gray matter settling to the bottom, and drinking it felt like wires drawn across the tongue.

From one blink to the next, the ringing quieted. Maeija inspected my face. I often wonder what she saw there.

Better, mayfly?

Before I could answer, Stig nudged a bowl of eel bones towards her newly emptied hands.

Well, what are you waiting for, beastie? Ah, never mind, I'll do it myself.

Stig beckoned me to escort him outside. We walked against the wind, our fists clenched against the warmth of our stomachs. In the shelter of a shivering linden, Stig tossed the bones in the snow and withdrew a clay pipe. I once owned its twin, both sculpted by Stig's uncle. It's long gone now. We stood apart from each other, teeth chattering.

Sure you can't wiggle up a spark of velti fire? He nudged me on the shoulder. I flinched. *The tea usually lasts longer, yeah? Or perhaps it's your brother's wanderings biting at your ankles? Don't waste a worry. Col could walk with Death under the hills and find his way back blindfolded.*

That's not an exaggeration. I still remember the first time Col invited me along to walk the curses with him. He made it seem so easy, striding into the unknown, feet barely touching the ground. I only made it a few miles before keeling over to empty the contents of my stomach. He hooted, not out of cruelty but for the simple joy of having me along. I didn't see it that way. After that, I avoided the curses, which meant avoiding Col. We became strangers to each other.

Which is to say, lingering outside the kitchens on that frozen morning, I wasn't thinking of my brother at all.

Despite all the tearstained promises made in the summer dark, the inequities between me and Stig had become unavoidable. Our boyish defiance snapped too easily under the heel of that imbalance. Although I reassured him it would be many, many years before I would receive my Blessing – ah, it hurts now to think how wrong I was! – he pled with me to refuse it.

I explained the Blessing was not simply a tradition, that without the mark to give release to the magic burning in my veins, it would eventually curdle both body and soul. Anyone who ignores the velti surrenders to the red hands of disease or despair.

And still, hearing all this, he continued to accuse me of selfish deformity!

We spoke in circles, grinding our arguments down to insults, to venom, to daggers. Did I suggest he should leave the Spire for various hells? And if I did, was it to hurt or liberate? I truly don't know. The forests of the past are unforgiving.

Well, plenty more fish to gut, Stig mumbled, the unlit pipe bobbing between his teeth. Then he clasped my hand and offered a startlingly genuine bow. The drumbeat of the velti pounded against my ribs. My last memory of him before he left Spire Iberos without word or warning was his gangly body slipping into the labyrinth of massive ovens with the ease of a fawn into the woods.

"I found it! Come on, stop dreaming. Wake up!"

Col stands over me, grinning madly, shards of pinking twilight caught in his hair. Before I can resist, he has me on my feet, a ratty cloak tossed over my shoulders. Insults curdle on my tongue before I remember his condition. Damn it. How is he standing? Where is he going? I push into my boots and chase him outside, past the fences and into the crackling frost. The trees thin out, their branches heavy with black leaves bowing inwards as we pass into the ephemeral corridor of the Grave-Green, one of the oldest curses.

Wheezing, he crouches in the snow. From above, I see lesions snaking down his neck, remnants of the latest huldufólk remedies.

"Let's go back," I say. "You can tell me about what you found, and I swear we can come back ... later in the season ... on a better day ..."

Col pulls himself back up. His eyes reflect the blood-dark spectrum of the sky.

He offers me his hand.

How can I refuse?

As we walk into the curs, the ground seems to speed from beneath us, as if every step doubles its distance. The trees whistle a strange tune. *Remember to breathe.* From Grave-Green, we pivot into other overlapping pathways – Serpents-Feast, Gallow-Seed, Ore-Fist, Tooth-Hook. The world fogs around us as we flicker, ghostlike, through wood and meadow, our feet barely touching the cobbled streets of distant Spires, our eyes blinking from flashing of rivers, lakes, sheets of ice crawling   down   the   mountain.

Occasionally, other travelers flit by us, women and men, Blessed and unmarked. I can still smell their skin long after their shades have passed. Perfume. Sweat. Wine. Disease. All of Casses flows through my lungs. *Remember to breathe.* At Col's insistence, we move faster and faster, until nothing remains other than buzzing smears of color. I cover my face with my hands, preferring the darkness.

"That wasn't so bad," Col says. He coughs into his hand and discretely wipes it under his arms.

The sun, returned a full hands-width up from the horizon, shines from a different direction. Instead of ice, the canopy drips with wet rubies of late autumn. It's difficult to determine exactly where we have alit; somewhere close to the southern rim I imagine. I begin to unpeel my cloak from the spreading tack of sweat, but Col stops me.

"Quiet. Listen."

The birds. Their song has changed from melody to keen. And there's this smell. Burning wood. The trees fall away as we step out onto a wide, rocky beach. The ocean surf inhales and exhales, pulling with it the smoke of a small campfire built at the edge of the tideline.

Two figures kneel before the flames, warming themselves. Col strides towards them, palms facing out in in friendly surrender, those damn manic teeth wide and bright.

"You wouldn't mind if my brother and I join you?"

I shuffle in behind him, an afterthought. As we near the fire, my eyes pull apart more details about the strangers; their odd, hunchbacked posture and stunted proportions.

A moment of panic seizes my chest.

Wild huldufólk. Not the servile creatures of the Spire. No, these hulda are proudly undomesticated — no rags conceal their wizened bodies, no attempt to meet the delicate standards of human agreeability. It is a stark reminder that these are the aboriginal inhabitants of this place, long before the Blessed and the shipwrecked. Their kind were here when Casses was a nameless rock and likely will be when it is again.

The larger hulda, a female, lopes over to Col. She draws a claw across his chest and sniffs it. For his part, he doesn't flinch.

"My friends, last we met you claimed knowledge of a hidden road," he says. "A way across the waters?"

Before they can answer, I pull Col aside.

"You've been here before? When?"

"I go where the velti leads me, little brother." He punctuates the last two words with an acidity that leaves me mute. He spins back to the hulda patiently waiting out our human melodrama. "Well? The curs?"

"Whale-Breath," nods the smaller creature. I notice that the tone and texture of his skin has changed to match the rocks beneath us. "I recall you paid the cheminage this time."

I watch with increasing trepidation as Col makes a show of wagging his fingers, clucking his tongue. The velti charges with an odor of overripe fruit. The hulda seems not to notice. With a snap, two silver coins appear in the air, already spinning in the light. Col rolls the coins up and down his knuckles like a street performer.

"A trick my mother taught me. Here's your toll."

The hulda pass the coins between themselves. Appeased, they snuff the fire and lead further along the coast, into the marshlands. It occurs to me that the landscape's contours are not entirely natural. What initially appears to be a mound of earth transforms into the underbelly of an overturned ship. The further inland we push, the more displaced vessels we pass, like abandoned toys in a dredged pond. I can trace the outline of their unusual prows beneath the vines, intricate sculptures of wood and iron — the fangs of serpents, the talons of eagles, a wyrm caught in metamorphosis. We hike around the broken face of an angel, slugs and beetles cozying between her stoic lips.

The migraine returns, pressing the thumbs of my eyes into my brain. I grab a branch from the ground and nervously roll it between my thumb and forefinger. My Blessing, brought to boiling by the velti fires in my skull, whittles away the wood like an axe, sharpening it to a knitting needle, a porcupine quill, a surgeon's pin. I hone it down to nothing, and the ache whittles away with it.

We arrive at a pair of obsidian sarsens rising out of the earth like the fingers of a buried god. Weathered runes swirl across them, a language I don't recognize. The hulda fall to their knobby knees and offer petitions to the massive stones. The sun is now just an amber shard snagged on dimming felt.

"Now what?" Col asks.

"You stepped between them."

Grinning madly, his molars grinding, Col walks forward between the sarsens. I wait for the bitter tang of the curs to sweep him away.

Nothing happens.

Col looks around, confused.

Then the hulda do something I've never seen before. They laugh.

It's horrifying.

Infuriated, Col tears the scarf away to reveal his mark. "I demand you reveal the curs to me. We are the Blessed. The open wounds of heaven!"

This only makes them cackle harder. They remind me of imps scribbled in the margins of a holy text.

"What do you want?" Col snarls. "What is it? More silver?"

His hands clench tight, gripping the velti so hard I feel it shift in my marrow. A coin falls from the sky and hits the sand with soft thud. Then another. And another. A clamor of raining metal fills the air as Col's deluge crashes around us, bouncing off the sarsens, breaking through the trees, pelting the shoulders and backs of the hulda. Their merriment pitches into hysterics as the rain becomes a gale, then a hurricane of silver.

I should try to pull Col away. I should beg him to stop.

With a word, I could end this.

Wait. Listen to the velti delighting in the music of its own song.

How could I ever deny him this moment of rapture?

Instead, I find a half-buried wreck and cower in its berth. I close my eyes and pretend the drum of coins against the wooden beams is the thunder of a summer squall.

The heavy rain slows, stops. A lone crow coughs into the widening silence.

"Judoc," Col says after some interminable time.

As we make our way back to the homeward curs, I hazard a quick glance back. The sarsens stand against the night like silent judges, passively watching over the unmoving shapes of the hulda. Then I turn my gaze back to Col, carefully reading the tremors rippling outward from the marrow of his shoulders, the rasping of his chest, the blood freckling across his chin. Ironic that for a miraculous moment, my own head is clean from pain. I can see every leaf turning white in the moonlight. I hear the pads of our feet, the movement of tiny insects, the fading breath of the endless, unrelenting sea.

While my mother accepted the pains, named them like pets, my father refused to acknowledge them.

His mark granted the gift of prosperity. Anything he touched thrived. Fruit trees. Wheat. Horses. Exotic orchids that had no right surviving through the Casses winters. His own children, born dark-haired and opal-eyed. He inherited a crumbling outpost and nurtured it into a beacon of opulence. Both Blessed and unmarked came to tend their gardens within our walls.

How quickly fecundity can turn cancerous.

Within a few years, thorny vines strangled the orchards. Gluttonous rats ate through our granary. The horses tore their ropes and disappeared into the woods. The orchids, so frail and delicate, gave birth to evil smelling tumors.

We had to burn it all.

Stig watches with curiosity as I light the candles, set out the linens and washing basins, wave away the cobwebs. Eir scuttles in with a decanter of wine, pungent with acorns and cloves.

Eir fills my glass, but ignores the other.

I raise my hand to the reprimand the hulda, but Stig gently restrains me.

"Come now, poor Adal is nearly blind with age."

"That's Eir."

"Oh, well, I could never tell them apart." He toasts me with his empty glass. "Now, I thought you didn't come up into the keep anymore. Just me and the spiders?"

A second pouring loosens my voice enough to tell Stig everything; the cackling hulda, the forest of shipwrecks, the storm of coins. He listens carefully until it's all spilled.

"You see ... Col's gift is to surface the lost and forgotten ... could be anything ... but he always comes back to the curses."

"Yeah, even as a wild-runt, I remember him being waist-deep in those weird roads. Can only imagine how it was after a Blessing like that. Did he find what he was looking for?"

"Yes," I say. "All of them. A completed map of Casses sits in his brain like a pulsing rot. So ... I suggested that perhaps there were some secret curs leading ... elsewhere. The gamble worked ... for a while ... but ... my efforts may have only thickened the poison ..."

"Easy, easy. You stutter as if you plucked the strings of his fate."

He means it as an absolution but it only pricks my temper.

As if cued, Eir returns with a pewter serving dishes balanced on root-gnarled elbows. The hulda spoons out fragrant servings of cooked fruit, again only for me, before scuttling back downstairs. I slide my plate over to Stig.

He smiles, teeth jeweled by candlelight. "I have something to show you."

He pulls a figurine from his pocket, a primitive bird-like totem, its silver feathers smoothed away by the centuries. His uncle claimed it was an ancestral heirloom, passed down from the survivors of the apocryphal landfall that introduced their bloodline to Casses. When no one was looking, Stig would steal it from its high shelf for our garden games.

"I took it before I left," Stig says. "Do you recall the hours we spent play acting with clay dolls from uncle's scraps? I would pluck a cob-spider to play the álfar, wicked prince of the small folk, and this was its witch-raven. And you would be the great and powerful sorcerer from the wild cliffs ... what was his name?"

"Lord Ormstunga."

"Yes! Serpent-Tongue! And you hunted down the álfar, threw it in uncles' kiln. We watched it burn until we couldn't take the heat. Remember? So, tell me, what is your Blessing, divine one? Can you drag down the stars? Can you reduce men to their bloody bones?"

I explain my gift to sharpen a thing to its finest edge. Metal, yes, glass, wood, a knife, a sword, a needle. Also, sight, a dream, a song. Joy. Grief.

"Ah, what a waste!" he exclaims. "So many dull knives could have used your attention back when I worked the kitchens. I snuck down there today, you know. Thought I'd pinch a flask of gray tea for you. What a sight. Ovens dead, pantries furred with dust."

His mention of Maeija's tea rattles craving's cage. I ease the conversation back to the missing years.

"I meant to prove my own way in the world," he says, biting into a steaming pear. "I was an idiot. Barely a month on the road and I blistered through two pairs of boots and nearly starved. It was a miracle that your cousin stumbled over me."

Bells ring deep in my ears, metal on bone.

"Mislav found you?"

He laughs. "Even before taking pity on my empty stomach, the old man shaved my head to clean out the ticks. When he realized I wouldn't be whimpering back home, he let me wander the wilderness with him. In return I shouldered his library and offered up my meager culinary skills. But, Judoc, let's not be coy. You don't really care about all that. You want to know about my mark. Been staring at it all night."

No reason to deny it. "Yes."

"I don't know if you recall the huldufólk Mislav traveled with. Vile, scheming little beasts. No doubt relatives of your tricksters in the woods. One night, I caught them sitting on his chest, suckling the velti from his mark as he slept. I had just been working a rabbit, still carrying the butcher knife. And. Well." He glances down at his scarred hands. The smile remains, but his words struggle like a moth in the rain. "You've not felt pain until you've been kissed by that blue fire they bleed."

Stig refuses to divulge any details, other than that when it was all over, the impossible had happened; his throat burned with the mark. Since then he's been traveling between the Spires, unlocking the secrets of this strange and inexplicable Blessing.

I ask him if the Blessing hurts. How he deals with the pain.

He acts as if he can't hear me. A sour draft whistles through cracks in the wall.

"Look. Here I am, to rescue you from this dour pile of rocks. Don't you see? We're the same now, nothing left to stop — oy! Be careful! Your hand!"

"What?"

Did I spill the wine? Bright drops of red roll off my fingers. No, not wine. There's a flap of skin hanging off my thumb, sliced neatly by the lip of the glass, whose edge I've idly sharpened to a near invisibility. Strange, how it doesn't hurt. The cut is too clean. Stig leaps from his chair and quickly wraps the wound with linen. Roses soak through.

"Here, let me help," he says, grabbing my hand. He concentrates on the injury. The velti gathers around him, not naturally like iron to the lodestone, but with great resistance. I can taste its resentment. Its loathing.

Finally, Stig gives up and runs downstairs, calling my brother's name. I try to follow him, but somehow end up going the wrong way, stumbling down the steps leading out into the courtyard. The frigid night jabs through the bloodied linen. I thrust my hand into the frost to numb the wound. Framed in the windows of the keep, the hulda glare down at me. From here, their faces are unreadable, statues in the moonlight.

When the paradise of Iberos began to rot, my family followed close behind.

Our father withdrew into himself, hoping that his inattention might restore nature's balance. But even abstinence tills our flesh into fertile soil for all manner of affliction. As with my mother, bone-fever took root in his velti's abscesses. As winter crept in, they became haunts of themselves, Lord and Lady of a fallen Spire.

Col spent more and more time away from home, walking the curses.

Stig and I remained inseparable, even as our quarrels grew teeth. Weeks went by without me speaking a single word to my parents.

When our cousin Mislav offered to relieve us of a few hulda, the decision was easy. At a whim, my mother gave him Vigdis, a spry imp from the gardens, and Maeija. From what I heard, they did not complain as he led them into the woods.

I was not there, of course.

It was the evening of Stig's disappearance.

I had retreated to the darkness of the keep, heartache and hatred crashing through me like lightning and thunder.

With the caress of morning's cold incandescence, Spire Iberos shudders into snappish wakefulness like a dog yet to slip into its housebroken mask. The few remaining inhabitants amble outside, women and men, half-dressed, snorting clouds of vapor, to dump the contents of their night buckets into the weeds or knock the icicles from their roofs. Some face down the rising sun with clenched lips. With neither Blessed nor hulda in sight, the unmarked bask in a world where merely human is enough.

Stig joins me at the window. He follows the activity below us with the genial indifference you might have for an ant crawling across your arm.

"Col is waiting for us in the next chamber."

"Then you've seen him in the daylight. The shaking, the bruises? It's just how my mother was, at the end."

"And when he's gone, what will you do?"

A roar kindles in my head, bells within bells. I grab Stig by the shoulders and shove him towards the exit. It's shocking to feel the warmth of his skin through his shirt.

"You haven't asked about your uncle."

"No."

"Ulcer-blossoms of the stomach," I sneer, tongue sharpened for cruelty. "Died sobbing and alone."

He flinches but doesn't budge. "Join us at the hearth. Bring your blankets. Col could use some more."

When our mother died, my father stood with us at the edge of the cremation pit. As both flesh and disease burned away, he refused to watch as Col breathed in the smoke, sucking it deep into his lungs, blacking his teeth to ashen gravestones. His eyes were showing their whites when the smoldering mark finally appeared on his throat. First, the stave for hunter, overlapped by the sign of the underground. Finder of the hidden and lost. His Blessing.

My father whispered something into the ear of his eldest son. Then he walked down into the fire. He didn't scream and he didn't look back.

Col rested his hands on my shoulders.

It was my turn.

I wasn't ready. I tried to run away, to do what Stig had begged of me so many times, to forgo family, destiny, to remain a child.

Col braced me and held my head into the grim cloud that my father was becoming.

Breathe, he commanded.

I struggled to twist out of his grip.

No!

He jammed his fingers into my mouth, gagging me. In that moment, with ashes crusting in my nose, I hated Col, a hate that still scratches at the back of my throat.

Breathe.

I had no choice but to relent to the fire and the cinders and the heat of velti released with my father's final heartbeats. His ashes filled me, Blessed me, marked me, and when I was sure I couldn't take any more was when my brother urged me to breathe deeper.

"And here comes our little Lord Serpent-Tongue," Col says.

Stig offers me a half-empty bottle of wine like the taper of a supplicant. When I don't move to take it, Col smirks and draws the blankets tighter around him. A bruise spreads across his face, dark as ink in the dim firelight. Several more of his teeth have fallen out.

Spots of dread whirl at the edge of my vision. How long have they been conspiring? A tight knot cannot be unraveled in the dark, but if enough hands tug the strings it may be undone by accident.

"Brother, let me help you back downstairs —"

Col glares at me. "No. You need to listen."

"To him?" I try to hide the urgency in my voice, even as the edges brighten, the pressure builds. "He's a kitchen boy who stumbled his way into his mark."

Stig runs a scarred finger around the bottles lip, making it sing. The spots pulse faster, dark feathers against my temple. "Transiency is the natural state of all things," he says. "Even the hardest, oldest stone is remade by a single drop of rain. It's a difficult lesson to learn." He passes his hand over the bottle, and the velti reduces it to a pile of quartz-glinted sand. "Or that might all be poetic nonsense. What do I know? Maybe you're right and all I'm good at is scaling a fish before it stops gulping for air."

Despair slips into the room like a ghost. It stares into the fire. Finally. I've been waiting for you. I don't care if the velti starves for attention, if it eternally pries its fingernails into the seams of my skull.

Nothing would make me happier.

Then another coughing fit rakes out from Col's lungs. Before his voice falls apart, he manages a hoarse whisper into my ear. "Don't you dare give up on me. Not yet."

After finally convincing Col to return to his bed, I peel back the wrappings around my thumb. The cut shines in its rawness. Some scabbing at the edges, the rest gapes like a drowning fish. Without asking, Stig inspects the wound for any slickness of infection. Why does such a simple act nearly bring me to tears?

I take my hand back and ask Stig why he believes he can save Col rather than be the final tap of false hope that nudges him over the edge.

As an answer, he produces a slight book, clasped in bronze, bound in pebble-gray reptilian leather. If my face betrays any reaction, he doesn't notice.

"It's an ancient war-tongue," he explains, tracing its spidery script. "Mislav claimed no knowledge of this book, that he had never set eyes on it before. Must have been a lie. Right? Yes. That's how I knew it was important."

"And he taught you how to read it?"

"No, he never had the chance. I taught myself – or, rather, I used my Blessing to transform into someone who always could read it. A small adjustment, really."

A small adjustment. That's how it always starts. Maybe just a taste, enough to prove it to yourself. A taste leads to a morsel to a meal to a bottomless feast, eat, eat or ache, eat or wither, until you realize, too late, that perhaps it's *you* that the velti has been devouring all along.

"There's a ritual described inside," Stig continues. "To carve out a new curs. It requires certain forms of velti, which we have between the three of us. And I know the perfect place to try it." He picked at the scars on his hands. "I'm sorry, should have told you right away. Not sure why I didn't."

"It's fine."

"Judoc, don't you think, now that we are both Blessed, there shouldn't be any more secrets between us? There doesn't need to be. Right? There's something I should tell you, about your cousin. Mislav, he didn't find me. I was waiting for him. I swear, I only wanted his guidance —"

Before he can speak another word, I take his damaged hands in mine. "It's fine."

With enough practice, any lie can be sharpened into the truth.

In all those years, away, did I think of you?

Stig, why don't you ask?

Then I could tell you.

Yes. Constantly.

I obsessed over you the way Col does his maps.

What you might look like, what you might be doing, where you might be. I saw you sleeping in a night-blue forest of pines. I heard you walking the marble streets of Spire Palus. I tasted the salt of the western sea on your teeth.

Visions of you sparked against a constantly spinning whetstone of resentment. I would wake up in the middle of the night, velti currents knotted in my hands.

I would tell you how strange it was, as Iberos collapsed, as my parents burned and my brother sank into desolation, that I remained healthy, even as I rarely exercised my Blessing.

How, in all that time, I never felt a drop of pain.

Not until the day you returned.

The tall grass snaps underfoot as we march through the fields. Our boots glitter with ice. We suck cold air through our teeth, where it warms along the roof of our mouths before rolling down into our lungs. Stig pauses occasionally to tug his cap back over his reddening scalp.

"Almost there," he says, multiple times, first as a joke, then more serious as familiar woodlands thin out to a horizon of cobalt stone. There is nothing alive out here, not a single sparrow, hare or beetle.

Col seems oblivious to the cold. Hope rouges his cheeks. I bet he's already imagining names for this new curs.

Approaching the mountains, the trail shakes off its snowpack to reveal crests of shale, uneven steps as likely to cast an unlucky traveler off as carry them forward. Up here, the hissing wind becomes more insistent. It seeks out any patch of exposed skin, groping at us, promising cool, dry kisses, if we only take off our cloaks, our scarves, our boots.

Stig pauses to gauge the way ahead.

"See those twin ridges of rock jutting out? My uncle called them the Sleeping Dogs. First time he brought me out here, I was certain that wolves or mud-snakes would devour us in the night. Nothing happened though. I suppose even devils find it too cold up here to bother."

Evening drops quickly. Other than a hazel shaft of sunlight pricking over the mountains, nightfall drains the world of color.

A coin flashes in Col's palm, then disappears again.

We reach a flattened palm of untouched snow sheltered between a copse of ice-heavy alder on one side and the elbow of a Sleeping Dog on the other.

There's a stillness here, the quietude of an ancient chapel, present and sacred, nature holding its breath.

We are exactly where we need to be.

"We best start," Stig says. "Before we lose the light entirely."

Col tastes the air. Nods. The lines of his body grow rigid, even the creases on his face, his grimace sharp as a scythe.

Stig sidles up to me and pulls my face close to his.

"Are you ready, divine one?"

He's giving me one more chance. To stop everything, to turn around and trudge back down the mountain and let events unfold as they should, a story already written where the Blessed of Spire Iberos fade away, our inheritance reclaimed by the ivy, the moss, the worms, our lineage forgotten to everyone except the huldufólk who had yet to meet us. Before our extinction, there might even be a time of warmth, rising from the decay in a rush of wine and tea, blood to blood, the sighs of aging friends.

And if I can see that possibility, so can Stig.

Above us, dark clouds churn through each other, trapped between the dusk and the mountains. As if driven by instinct, we concentrate our Blessings. The velti responds. Even as the pain flickers away, I start to say something, I can't even tell what, a dozen shapeless words rising from my ribs, when the sun goes rust and velti wildfire leaps from Col's throat, to Stig's, to mine. Magic pops and spurts between us, burning away our emotions, its alchemy shifting the elements to air, to water, to glass.

I was a babe when Maeija came to me.

She looked then exactly as she does now, as she probably did when the earth itself slipped the fiery cowl of its birth. She crept into my chambers in the middle of a moonless night with what would be the first of many cups of gray tea. As my headache dulled, she climbed up onto my bed. I will never forget the jab of her knees through the blankets. The smell of her breath, like the heavy air from a cavern deep underground. The rough brush of her bark-scaled lips against my ear.

There, as I laid in the darkness, paralyzed by terror, she related the entirety of my life, backwards.

You rose from a broken corpse, she said, *up, up, into the keep, through that very window on the other side of this room. The sickness shook you like a doll, softer and softer, through a winter and a summer. Then you barely felt the fever at all, other than a twinge in your jaw. Yes, just like you see in your mother's jaw now. Then, your brother walked out of the ocean, relief turned to anger, to despondency. He can barely remember being dead, all those guts eaten by crabs. He rejoined you here in the Spire for many years, some happy, others less so. The bone-fever burned brightly in him, before fading, before your mother and father pulled themselves out of the ashes ...*

Please, enough, I wept. *I don't want to know this.*

Don't be frightened, mayfly. It is a story already told, a stone resting at the bottom of the sea.

It's horrible.

She drew her claws through my hair, gentle as a kitten.

Perhaps, together, we tipped the stone as it settled? Speak truthfully. What else could you have done for your own blood? Was it all worth it to take away their pain?

All I had was family. They were my whole world. Even Stig, despite all his charms, could never grasp the beautiful and terrible magic that stitched the Blessed together in threads of white and black.

Anything, I said. *I would do anything to save them.*

In that way, we were the same. She pressed a thin book into my hands. It felt oddly alive. I swear there was a fading pulse under its skin. *This came back to me in the cage of a corpse. It wrote itself. You slipped it in with others of its kind. You chose a darling of unlike blood carry it. You kept it hidden for a hundred turns of the moon.*

As she climbed off my bed, I asked her how this could possibly save my family.

Left alone, a quiet love retained its simple form. Hit with an axe, it shattered to dust. But, carefully fletched, whittled over time, you turned a green sapling to a needle, its life sharpened to pierce the world's skin.

Me? I will cure them? That is to be my Blessing?

It was too dark to see, yet I knew she was grinning.

Mayfly, that was my weapon.

Stig screams into the unnatural gale swirling around us.

"Col, now!"

My brother, weak, skeletal, raises his hands into the velti. It appears first as a smudge, then a shadow, then a shape. Massive. Dark. It crashes to the ground and I recognize it as one of the obsidian sarsens from the forest of shipwrecks. It totters precipitously over us like a finger about to crush a beetle, before settling into the snow. The second sarsen arrives with a thunderclap, taking its place by its twin.

Col collapses in exhaustion, tongue lolling.

I look over to Stig. He's concentrating on the empty space between the sarsens. Under his guidance, the air dulls like a cataract, softening the sharp angles of the mountains beyond. With a final grunt of effort, he becomes midwife to a shivering curs that limps and lurches out from the gap.

The velti seethes around us. Col grimaces, lips wet with bile.

"Behold," he cries triumphantly, "I name thee the Broken-World curs."

It is not complete. To enter now would be like walking into oblivion.

A tempting thought.

According to the book, three Blessings are required to create a new curs. Col's gift of finding brought the sarsens to this location. Stig changed history, making it as if this end of the curs were always tethered to the stones.

As for reaching the other side …

Stig hands me the bird-like totem, our witch-raven, the relic of a distant continent. Sparks roll down its silver wings.

I take the totem and roll it between my velti-slicked palms until it softens like wax, keep spinning until it forms a rod, then a spear. With shaking hands, I aim the tip towards the curs. The velti wind draws it forward as if pulled by a string.

The curs ripples at the impact. But it does not open.

I knew it wouldn't.

"Oh," Stig says.

"Your uncle probably thought it was real."

Col has curled up in a soft pile of snow rusted with vomit. He's barely breathing.

"It's over," I say. "Help me carry him home. Better to die in his own bed than out here."

Stig looks to Col, then to me.

Many strains of acquaintance may sprout in the thin soil of our footsteps; comradery, love, lust. Friendships blossom like wildflowers. However, a perfect bond, a heart that returns to your side through seasons of pain and selfishness? One that, when presented with the opportunity, would choose to sacrifice itself for your own happiness? Infinitesimally rare. Like my father's impossible gardens, it must be meticulously cultivated. Take a scythe to the weeds, to the stragglers, to the less desirable offshoots. Creation is an act of cutting away all other possibilities.

"Something else we can try ..."

There's a thousand things I should say now. I have been practicing them all my life.

Stig, perhaps, once, you truly were a friend to a monk who found you in the woods. Perhaps, once, he died peacefully in his sleep, and you stood too close to his funeral pyre. A smudge of the velti singed your throat. Enough to taste. To want more. To abandon what you were and eventually, through slaughter and desperation, to dream yourself to my equal.

Stig, you always were my equal.

Stig, don't make me choose.

Stig, the truth is, I chose this a long time ago.

My lips refuse to speak, even as Stig embraces me and his mouth covers mine, as his breath fills my lungs, as he draws the velti from me, Ormstunga, Serpent-Tongue. He already understands. Perhaps he knew from the moment I agreed to come to this barren place. What portion of our lives is constructed from such feints to ignorance, burying our wet natures to play the roles required? We tell ourselves we can step off the stage at any time. But controlling our story takes an act of creative violence, one whose expanding design refuses easy perception, even as it alters everything it touches.

While it's undeniable that all humans are alien to Casses, via some unnatural symbiosis the Blessed anchored themselves to this rock. Stig's people never had that chance. We bound their identity to exclusion. Their blood. Shipwrecked. Unmarked.

He is the shape hidden in the wood.

I am the blade with which to carve it out.

"Wait," is all I manage to say before the velti reads our intent and explodes with a prehistoric wail, rooting out from the marks in our throats, encircling us, forcing us closer, pressing my hands to his chest, then sinking into his chest, one knuckle, two. He buckles as his knees fuse together. His ribs explode outward, the bones jutting from the skin in a spray of red. A sheen of moss crawls upwards from where his feet used to be, bursting from the muscles beneath. That's when he finally screams.

Ever since Maeija's prophecy, I have only prayed for one thing; that this moment would be painless.

I should have known better.

Stig, my darling. This is our Blessing.

His face is last to transform. His eye sockets pinch shut. Teeth crack. Muscles harden. He has become a milestone of bone and flesh. As the velti lifts him up and carries him into the white maw of the curs, I can still see a hint of his smile in the scratching runes.

The Broken-World curs erupts into brilliance. A corridor of light pours out like a crimson thread from the needles eye. It effortlessly flows across the rough, between the ears of the Sleeping Dogs, presumably crossing the mountains and the ice freckled waters beyond.

Through the warped glass of the curs, plagues of flies rumble over a wasteland of sand and vermillion scrub. No, not flies, distant warships, floating in the air. Entire armadas of those carved totems skate across the surface of a burning horizon, just as my mother did, that effortless glide. Will they become the wrecks in the marshlands? Am I seeing the past or the future?

It doesn't matter.

Pain exists outside of time.

The curs warbles. Something emerges from the other side. It is difficult to look at. My eyes slide off its shifting collection of limbs, arms and legs, intertwined with serpentine roots of gaslight. It takes no heed of me or Col as it picks through the snow, constantly changing shape, shrinking, hardening, a liquid mandala becoming stone.

I know what this is.

Prince of the small folk. Mythic creature of pure velti.

Álfar.

It pauses at the bloody pile of rags that were Stig's clothes. A sinuous claw plucks the leather book out from the carnage and gently attaches it to a weeping sore of matching shape on its flank.

Then it sees me.

Orbs of blue flame flicker in its sockets.

"Judoc of Iberos. Your life made a nice splash dropping into the pond of time, mayfly."

My mouth goes numb with the taste of gray tea.

"Maeija?"

"A good name. Perhaps I will take it one day."

A thousand questions sting my tongue to silence. All I can manage is stutter.

The álfar whispers into my ear.

"The knife in its velvet sheath needed not know why it was made, or in whose forge it was birthed. It only needed to know how to cut."

A second phantom steps through the curs, then a dozen more, a hundred, an upended waterfall of thrashing shadows pouring from the curs and spilling across the mountains. Horror clamps my ribs. Is this an invasion? A plague?

A reclamation?

An invisible wind takes them up, light as spiderlings, and carries them into the night. As fast as they arrived, they are gone. Gone into our dead past, their future.

Stars prick through the thin clouds.

I crawl over to Col and press my ear to his chest. Still breathing. I leverage him over my shoulder and make my way towards the curs. My arms brush against the milestone. It is warm, slightly yielding. It reminds me of when Stig and I sat on our hands and watched his uncle work the sculptor's wheel. It always fascinated me to see a simple lump of clay transformed by nothing other than his naked hands. He didn't need the velti to infuse the inanimate with grace and beauty. Once, he sculpted us miniature replicas of ourselves, perfectly detailed down to the fingernails. I remember Stig cradling his brittle boy in his hands. I remember crushing mine under my heel, not for the sin of accepting gifts from the unmarked, but for the unfairness of it being unfeeling clay all the way through.

I drag my brother's limp body past the milestones, into the curs, toward the ragged dawn of a distant shore.

About the story

This story began with the image of a two men standing before a gate in the mountains. At their feet was a body, crumpled in the snow. I knew the two men were brothers. The body remained a mystery until I heard someone define "cheminage" on the radio, as an old word for a toll to pass through the forest. That's exactly what the body was. Everything else flowed from the tension of that triangle and the strange red sky on the other side of that gate.

A question for the author

Q: What kind of pieces are the most fun to write (action, lyrical, etc.)?

A: The human mind has an underrated capacity for acceptance. The pieces I find the most fun to write are those that arise from characters placed in unexpected, uncomfortable or even horrific situations and then watching them navigate their way through it. No matter how dark or bizarre the circumstances, the act of living always finds its own lyric beauty.

About the author

David Gallay is a writer of speculative fiction and horror. After receiving a B.A in Creative Writing from Binghamton University, and currently resides in

Wisconsin where he leads a double life as an IT SysAdmin.

@svengali

Hold This Star For Me

Mark David Adam

When David got to work that morning, he discovered a large shell on his desk holding down errant pieces of paper. He smiled. His coworkers were always razzing him about how messy his desk was and now, it seemed, someone had taken it upon themselves to assist him.

He picked up the seashell; it was as big as his fist. It didn't have pointy bits like a conch but was smooth, almost like a marshmallow that had been melted and stirred then set again.

He lifted the shell to his ear, something he had not done since he was a boy. He half expected the old notion that you could hear the ocean in an empty shell to have gone the same way as the Easter bunny and other childhood things, but he did hear waves, like the whispering of a giant.

He closed his eyes and found himself thinking of a beach side motel he and his mother had stayed at when he was around six. He hadn't thought of that time in years but now an unusually vivid memory rose in him. It was of standing on the beach, listening to the crash of waves, while sand blew against his legs. The sand had felt like the pricks of insect bites and as a child he had been confused by this. He had seen bugs, ugly bugs, hopping out of a washed up tangle of kelp he'd poked with a stick. He hadn't seen the bugs clearly, been too repulsed to get too close, but he had dimly seen, or perhaps imagined, that they had tusks of all things, and in his mind that meant they should be much larger than him not jumping about at his feet. When he felt the pricks of the sand he had thought they were the same bugs, now even smaller.

He opened his eyes and laughed, recalling how he had screamed and cried, telling his mother giant shrunken bugs were eating him.

That night, laying in bed, reflecting on how different his thinking and perception had been as a child, he had the growing feeling there was another memory in him wanting to surface. As sleepless hours went by, he became more and more convinced that something else had happened at the motel, something that — unlike the crawling insects and blown sand which he could reconfigure with an adults understanding — would be more strange if remembered now, not less. A child's whole world is largely of unknowns. He could, he was sure, have witnessed something and not seen it for what it was, a truly unusual event.

When dawn arrived before sleep he got up, sent a message to work saying he wouldn't be in, then drove to his mother's, arriving in time for lunch.

"I can't recall," his mother said, taking the kettle off the stove.

"I think I was six," he said. "So I guess it was before we moved here." He thought about how the wind had been cold; had it been early spring or fall?

His mother set a tea pot on the table.

"A motel?" she asked, turning back to the cupboard and taking out a package of Peek Frean cookies. She shook the package before opening the top and looking inside.

"It was on the ocean," he said. He had a clear image in his mind. "There were sliding glass doors and just a bit past the back deck you could walk to the beach."

"Oh, you must mean Taylor Bay," she said, opening the trash can and throwing the empty package out.

"No," he replied.

"You used to love going to Taylor Bay," she said, opening another cupboard.

"It wasn't Taylor Bay."

"You sure David? You were quite young, weren't you?"

He knew it wasn't, and if his mother thought about it at all, she would know that not only had they never stayed at Taylor Bay, there were no motels there.

He didn't think too much of this discrepancy in recall with his mother. She had never been one for details or direction. Even now, after having lived in the same house for twenty years, she could get disoriented and find herself driving out of town instead of to her local shopping centre. And she still told her friends that he'd studied anthropology at university, her memory sealed by his description of an early course he had taken.

David took a sip of tea and wondered if his mother's poor recall had inspired him to look more closely at his own memories. He didn't think so; it didn't explain the pull he felt.

The next morning, while waiting to pay for fuel at a gas station, he pulled a road map off a rack and examined it, but the lines of highways and names of towns did not evoke anything. Back in his car he found himself driving towards the coast. He didn't think it likely that the motel, which he remembered as being old back then, would still be there. Still, he always had liked road trips and the possibility of finding the same beach excited him.

And then, after a morning of driving through forests and farmlands, it happened.

He rounded a corner and the highway broke through to an open view of the sea from atop a high cliff. As he began his descent to the coast, he recognized the bay below him, remembered seeing it for the first time as a young boy. He felt this so strongly it was as if his younger self was riding in the car beside him.

He remembered rolling down his window (his mother had complained about her hair getting in her eyes) and sticking his head out, imagining he was flying over the ground like superman.

He smiled, opened his window, extended his hand, and moved it like a rolling wave against the rushing air.

After many switch backs, the road levelled out and he drove past houses, cabins, craft stores, a gas station, and motels. And yes, after he had driven the whole length of the bay, he found *the* motel.

The sign, which he had had absolutely no memory of a moment before, he immediately recognized. He remembered looking at it while waiting in the car as his mother went inside. It was of a large seahorse, painted gold and green: the Seahorse Motel.

He pulled in and peered at the buildings in front of him. He could see now that he had not remembered it right. He had thought it had been like most motels, one long building with adjoining rooms, but it wasn't. There were three small cottages that he could see, possibly more behind.

The place was not well kept. The paint on the cottages was sun bleached and flaking. Some of the pale roof tiles on the cottage in front of him had come loose, revealing their original colour beneath to have been a dark green. And there were dandelions everywhere. They rimmed the foundations of the cottages and flowed out over the gravel parking lot as if they were running from under the buildings, attempting to flee.

He looked past the cottages; unable to see the ocean he opened his door and got out.

Wind, not strong but full and steady, blew off the ocean, cool like it had been in his memory. His sense of smell had never been strong, but he had no problem perceiving the scent of the sea. And he heard it, the low thrush of waves falling on sand.

He walked to the end of the parking lot, stepped onto an old log, and looked at the horizon. The sun was low, hidden in clouds far out from land. The sea was not blue, but reflected the clouds above; it was the colour of concrete and appeared tired. Everything was so muted he felt like an actor in a black and white film.

He heard a screen door bang shut behind him. Turning he saw a man walking towards him.

When the man was about ten feet away he stopped. He gazed above David's head as if examining something. David turned, wondering if perhaps a bird had caught the man's interest, but somehow he didn't think so, and looking he saw nothing in the sky. When he turned back, the man came closer.

"Hello," the man said, his eyes the blue the sky and water should be.

"Hello," David replied.

"You looking to stay?"

He had not had time to think of that.

"You have a cottage available?"

The man waved his hand.

"Take your pick," he said. "The newer motels drop their rates at this time of year and the few people who come through at this time stay elsewhere. I can let you stay for half our usual."

David made a show of looking around, but he already knew he would.

David slid back the glass door and let the wind and the sound of the sea enter the cottage. The deck before him looked small, but he was certain this was the same cottage he had stayed in as a boy. Before him, dandelions seemed to be in conflict with another plant. A single golden flower grew up through a tangle of wild succulents, while other dandelions watched from around the edge of the cottage. Were the dandelions advancing? he wondered. Or was this other foliage? Was the lone dandelion making headway into indigenous terrain, or was it the first to be attacked by invaders from the shore?

It didn't appear, as he drove looking for a place to eat, that there was any real town. There was no shopping centre, no grocery or drug store. The gas station where he stopped to refuel had a few shelves on which, besides the usual chips and chocolate bars, sat two lonely loaves of white bread and various summer-time condiments. The fridge held ice and pop, a single carton of eggs, and empty racks where a twisted sign indicated wieners had been displayed and probably would be again when summer returned. He was told by the teenager behind the counter that he would have to drive half an hour south to buy more substantial fare. Similarly, the first restaurant he came across was closed, and the second. He drove the whole length of the bay until at the end he found one that was open.

It did not look promising.

Walking up to the front doors David saw only one other parked car, and the motel the restaurant was attached to showed no signs of activity. He was not greeted by people or sounds when he entered. He walked past an unmanned reception desk and down a narrow unlit hallway till he emerged into a surprisingly bright and pleasant room. The front wall was not straight but curved like the prow of a ship, with full windows facing towards the ocean. Outside, the horizon glowed softly. It was not a vivid and spectacular sunset. No rays pierced the clouds, which held only the slightest tinge of orange, but it was beautiful in a calm, assured way.

A man sat at a table facing the view, a glass of beer in his hand. His light hair looked like a crashing wave caught in a photo; it rolled up off his forehead, gaining height as it drifted towards the back of his head. David heard a cup connect with plate and turned to his left. Another man, fingers pinched delicately through the small handle of a coffee cup, was staring at him, as was the man who sat across from him. They both had on dark suits, not expensive, nor had they recently seen the inside of a dry cleaner. The men did not nod a greeting, nor go back to their half eaten pies, but stared at him unblinking. David imagined that if he had a better sense of smell, he would be able to detect a lingering touch of embalming fluid emanating from them.

He moved towards a table on the other side of the room, but as he passed the man with wavy hair, he saw that the table next to him also had a better view of the setting sun.

As David sat down, the man turned and looked at him lazily, or perhaps drunkenly, his smile friendly enough, and a sharp contrast to the two men at the table behind, who had swivelled their heads and were still watching him intently, unconcerned or unconscious of being rude.

"Hello," David said to the man with wavy hair as he sat down.

"Hello," the man said, pointing his beer towards him before lifting it to his mouth. The man looked at David while he drank, keeping his eyes on him until his beer, which had been half full, was all gone. When the man had finished drinking, he put his glass down, smiled as if at some private reminiscence, then startled David by bellowing out, "Sarah."

This produced no immediate results, but after several long moments, moments in which the man continued to hold his gaze, David heard footsteps in the hall.

Over the man's shoulder, he saw a woman around his own age enter the room, her dark hair close on either side of her face, like stage curtains closing. She wore a simple, light blue dress and had a beer in one hand, evidently familiar with the wants of the man who had yelled.

The woman stopped when she saw David, stopped like a bird hitting glass.

The men in suits swivelled their heads between her startled stance and David.

It was for only a moment that the woman stood still and their eyes connected, but that moment seemed larger and fuller than the time accorded it. If he were to learn it had lasted centuries unchanging, waiting for the machinery of time to begin to roll again, he would not have been surprised.

The woman walked past the men at the table and it seemed to David that he saw a flicker of fear in her eyes and that her shoulders were taut in the anticipation of trouble.

She placed the beer in front of the man beside David, picked up his empty glass and held it lightly, as if weighing its potential as a weapon.

"Perhaps this man would like a menu," the man said reaching for his beer, "or a drink."

"Kitchen's closed," she said.

The man turned to her. "Surely a sandwich is in the realm of possibility. He appears to have travelled far."

Sarah looked down. The room, as when he had first entered, as when she had first entered, was thickly silent. Words, footsteps, were the anomalies, allowed, but visitors with few rights.

Sarah lifted her gaze back to David. This time, instead of fear, her eyes narrowed and her mouth tightened with what he thought was a trace of anger.

"I don't want to be a bother," he said quietly.

Their eyes locked.

In David's mind there appeared a scene of being at the beach, of patting a small, blue, upside down pail with his hands and then lifting it gingerly to reveal a compressed tower of sand. A hand, not his, came into view and placed a shell on top.

"I can make a sandwich," she said.

"That would be nice."

"Roast beef?"

He nodded.

"Anything to drink?"

"Could I have some tea?"

"Regular?"

He nodded again. In his mind he saw a hand holding thin seaweed, the kind of sea weed that you can almost see through when you hold it up to the sun. The hand placed the sea weed around the base of the small sand tower.

She turned away; her thin dress billowing slightly as she did so. She walked past the men at the table, who had not stopped staring. One was slowly lifting a sliver of pie towards his mouth. His eyes on the woman, his aim was low; the fork hit his lip as she walked past. The man pushed the piece of pie into his mouth, then turned to David with blue smeared lips.

David adjusted his chair so that it pointed away from the men at the table and out at the view. As he sat waiting for his sandwich, he was unsure if the silence was more uncomfortable than it would be to have a conversation with the man beside him considering the audience they had. When the man did not speak, but stared as raptly at the ocean as he had before, David followed his example.

When Sarah returned with his sandwich and tea, she placed them on the table without speaking. She also brought another beer for the man, at which he smiled and drained the one in his hand. When David had finished half his sandwich, he heard the rub of chairs on the floor behind him. He did not turn and look. He was certain the men in suits were standing, staring at him. He took two bites of his sandwich before he heard footsteps walking away and then he did turn, making sure that the men in crumpled suits were truly gone. He wanted to comment to his neighbour on the men's strange manner, but the words did not come to him. He looked towards the man beside him who, continuing to stare out the window at the sea and sky, much darker than they had been, said, "Maybe tomorrow night?"

Before David could answer, or even begin to speculate on what this meant, the man stood, held his beer up to the departed sun, drank the last of it, then turned and walked out.

The woman, Sarah, did not return.

When David had eaten his sandwich and drank his tea, he got up and called tentatively into the hall. There was no response. He sat back down, tested the small stainless teapot she had brought to see if there was anything left and, discovering it empty, got back up.

"Hello," he called again into the hall.

He walked to the reception desk.

"Hello," he tried again.

When no one answered, and he heard no sound of movement, he returned to the dining room, took out a ten dollar bill — it was either that or a twenty and he did not feel the dry sandwich and tea deserved it — and placed it under a knife beside his plate and left.

At his car, he turned and looked back. He wasn't sure, but the curtains of an upstairs window moved as if a hand had been holding them to the side and had just let go.

Sleep did not come easily. The bed was harder than he liked, and cold; it took a long time for his body to warm the sheets. He did like the sound of the ocean though, and the absence of the city noises he usually heard in his apartment.

When he woke, he lay in bed trying to remember his dreams. He felt they had been important. There was something about a door but, in the way of dreams, the door, while being a door, had been something other too, like a cat or a tree.

It was a sunny day. Once he got up, he sat on the cottage's back step, rolled up his pant legs, then walked onto the beach barefoot. As bright as it was, he discovered that it was still quite cool and walking barefoot was not as enjoyable as he had hoped it would be. He did venture into the water though, remembering as a child laughing at the feel of outgoing waves eroding the sand beneath his feet. The tide was advancing, though, not retreating, and the sand beneath him stayed firm, while the icy water felt as if it were cutting his skin.

He walked back to the cottage dejected, but not inconsolably so. He decided go into town, have breakfast, come back and explore again properly attired.

As he made his way up from the beach past a ribbon of driftwood to where clumps of succulents appeared like small islands in the sand, a voice called out to him. He hadn't expected to be addressed and at first thought the wind was sending him sounds meant for someone else. Looking up, he saw the man who had rented him the cottage gesturing to him, his movements overly dramatic, as if the two of them were in the midst of gale force winds and he was offering sanctuary.

"Hello," the man said when David had walked up sufficiently close to hear. "Would you like some coffee?"

He did want some coffee, though he stood for a moment without speaking. Here, away from the water, the sand was drier. It blew against his legs and he felt tiny pricks along the back of his calves.

He smiled.

The man smiled back. He had a softness to his face and David sensed a loneliness in him, a long, well-established loneliness.

"Coffee would be great," David said. "I haven't had a chance to get any groceries."

"Come in, come in," the man gestured, again too largely, his arms moving as if they were pulling in a net.

David followed the man stepping up through the sliding door at the back of his cottage.

"Here," the man said, extending a towel towards him with which to wipe his feet. "How do you like your coffee? Cream? Sugar?"

"Black would be fine."

When he was done wiping the sand and moisture from his feet, David looked around the room. Shelves extended from floor to ceiling along one whole wall, filled with all manner of things. David found himself squatting down. On a low shelf, sticking out from behind a piece of driftwood, was a thin gold rod the length of his hand and just slightly wider in diameter than an ink tube from inside a pen.

He picked the rod up. It was light, but he sensed that it would not bend to any pressure his hands could give.

"Here you…"

David looked up. The man, holding a cup of coffee in each hand, was staring at the rod in David's fingers, his mouth open in mid-sentence. David felt that by holding the object he had invaded the man's privacy, had broken ancient rules of guests and hosts.

He did not replace the small rod on the shelf, however. He stood up holding it. The man backed up a few steps, his mouth still hanging open.

Feeling uncomfortable, David turned from the man and looked at the shelves.

Why had he been drawn to this one object out of all that were there before him? At eye level was a beautiful purple spiral of a worn shell, beside it a full wing of a dark feathered bird. Why, and how, had he seen the object that was in his hand? Certainly his eyes should have gravitated towards these other more noticeable and attractive objects first. And now that he looked at the items on the shelves more closely, he saw that what at first he had assumed to be simply interesting pieces of driftwood, were in fact subtly carved. The knots and grains of weather moulded wood had been delicately emphasized, causing faces and animals and birds to appear like shy hallucinations. He knew the man had carved them; they echoed the loneliness David sensed in him. He wished now that he had noticed these figures first and commented on the skill they evinced, but he hadn't, and looking back at the man, he saw it was too late now. There were tears in the man's eyes and — David was not entirely sure if he was imagining it or not — the thin rod in his hand was vibrating with a soft current.

The man composed himself and stepped forward, holding out a cup of coffee.

David took it.

The man kept his hand extended. David looked down at the rod in his hand, then reluctantly gave it to him.

The man slid his hand inside his jacket, depositing the rod into a pocket, then patted his chest over top of where it was.

"She gave it to me and told me to look after it," he said as if this explained everything.

They went outside, sat on low beach chairs, and drank their coffee watching crows along the tide line scratch the sand with their claws and peck at it with their beaks, feeding on creatures buried beneath.

"I had forgotten," the man said after a time. "Well, not forgotten, just stopped thinking about it."

He looked out towards the horizon.

"It's been so long," the man said quietly.

Sitting beside this man, David felt as if he were at the bedside of a loved one in a hospital. He didn't know what to say, but felt it was important he was there.

After David had drunk his coffee, and the cup was becoming cold in his hand, the man spoke again.

"I don't think they remember either," he said sadly. "Things..." his hand fluttered as if picked up by the breeze, "things distract and over time bury the past."

The man looked at David, seeming to need some response. Not knowing what to say, David nodded.

"But you," the man said smiling. "You're here."

David smiled back.

After another long period of silence, David got up.

"Thank you for the coffee," he said.

He stood in front of the man and held out his hand. Like the man's earlier emphatic gestures, the man shook his hand in overly large up and down strokes before stopping and squeezing David's hand firmly.

"Don't let him fool you," the man said looking him in the eye. "He's as dangerous as he ever was."

He went to fetch his mother. He had been exploring the beach and at first that had been preferable to waiting in the cottage for his mother to shower and drink her coffee, but after awhile he felt too alone. It was not enough to chase gulls and cause them to fly; he needed to be seen doing so. It was not enough to be the only one to look at the things he found. He needed his mother to also hold the tiny spirals of broken shells and wonder with him. It was uncomfortable to see something beautiful or interesting on his own; he didn't know how to contain it. So he walked back to the cottage holding some of his best finds: a dried out baby crab fully intact, a piece of rounded green glass, and an oyster shell with sea weed attached to it, looking like a withered hand.

When he was close to the cottage he saw his mother sitting outside, not on a chair, but on the ground, leaning against the sliding glass door, her knees drawn up and her arms resting on them. He called out to her as he approached, excited to show her what he had in his hands. Her head turned so slowly towards him that he in turn slowed his pace and then, when he was still twenty feet or so away, he stopped entirely.

He had never seen his mother, or any adult, cry before. He had not known it was something they did. He did not know how to respond. His mother did not say anything, did not rise to greet him. She looked at him for a moment then leaned her head against the glass behind her and closed her eyes.

It frightened him.

He stood there lost, not able to go to her and not able to leave.

He felt a tug on his shirt.

A girl, a few years older than him, motioned with her hand and, not knowing what else to do, he followed her back to the beach.

They walked until they came to a log, its trunk buried in the sand as if it had been thrown there by some giant. The roots stuck out above the ground and someone had placed a stone in the centre of them, making an eye, turning the sun bleached log into a dragon, its roots now whiskers and teeth, horns and scales.

"Here," the girl said, holding out a plastic blue pail. "Go get some wet sand."

David carefully put down the things he was carrying and did as he was asked.

Later, after he had made a ring of towers and she had decorated them with sea weed and shells and feathers and he had not thought of his mother for quite some time, the girl surprised him by saying, "She wasn't crying because of you."

That thought had never occurred to him.

"She was crying because of your father."

"My father?"

"He's a bad man."

"He is not," David said, feeling attacked.

The girl did not reply, and after a moment David looked up from his moat digging to find her staring at him.

"My father's a bad man too," she said.

David did not know if his father was a bad man, did not think so, but the way she looked at him, he wanted his father to be. He wanted to share this grown-up like seriousness with her.

"My father's a very bad man," the girl said, placing a feather on the castle wall, "and like your mother, I have to do something about it."

He did not go into town for groceries like he'd planned. The thought of leaving the bay and entering the outside world not only did not appeal to him, he felt it might endanger his quest. The past, like a hungry feral cat, was showing itself, but that it would continue to do so was not certain.

He spent the day alternating between strolls. First to the point south of the motel and then, after stopping back at the cottage, where he made himself some tea he found in the cupboard, he walked north towards the end of the bay, but not all the way. He did not want to go as far as the restaurant. Not yet.

After his second, longer walk, he lay on the bed in his cottage and it was then he had remembered meeting the girl and building the sand castle.

And then, standing at the sink, filling a glass with water, looking out at the ocean, an image had surfaced in his mind of her dark hair blown back in the wind as he ran to keep up with her longer legs.

"My father says it's time for us to leave."

"No," he said, grabbing her arm and making her stop.

She looked at him.

"You're right," she said. "We mustn't let him leave. Will you help me?"

He nodded.

"It's....dangerous," she said.

"That's OK," he replied.

She took his hand in hers and squeezed it.

He took a deep breath and felt himself grow larger inside.

When David drove to the restaurant, the same lone car was in the parking lot that had been there the day before and the reception desk was still as lifeless as a museum exhibit.

"Do you like fish? Halibut to be exact?" the man with the wavy hair said the moment David stepped into the dining room.

"Uh…Yes," David answered.

"Good, good," the man nodded. "Caught today by our skilled and dedicated neighbour. Rice? A white marinade sauce?"

"Uh.."

"No. You're right," the man said, jabbing the air with his finger. "Why cover up the natural flavor? Grilled, that's it. With potatoes. Yes, and some pickled cabbage on the side for contrast and digestion." He rubbed his hand in circles across his stomach at the last word.

"Sit."

The man pointed to the table David had eaten at the night before, then disappeared down the hall, singing as he moved away. The man's voice trailed off, then became loud again as he returned with a beer and a glass and put them on the table.

David looked at them.

"On the house," the man said, patting David's shoulder. Singing again, he turned and left.

When there was only an inch of beer left in his glass, and the sun was a similar visual distance above the horizon, David heard footsteps behind him. He turned, hoping it would be Sarah, but it was the men in suits. They looked at him like he was a strange animal, or perhaps like they were strange animals. They made their way to the same table they had been at the night before. They continued to stare at him as they sat down. The one who had smeared pie on his lips the day before collided with the side of the table. He did not stop looking at David as he slid his hip along the table's edge and lowered himself into a chair.

David found that he was not as disturbed by the men as he had been the night before. He felt no ill intentions towards him from them.

Moments after their arrival, the man returned, expertly carrying five steaming plates, two plates in each hand and one balanced on the crook of his arm. He stopped at the table with the men in suits, who each took a plate, and then came over to David and placed the rest.

"Sarah!" he yelled as he had the night before. The man looked and saw David's nearly empty beer. "Ah yes," he said, and walked away, calling out "Sarah" again when he was in the hallway.

The man returned with a beer in each hand and sat down.

"Bon appetit," he said, toasting David.

David had never thought it before, but he wondered now if his poor sense of smell meant he also had a diminished sense of taste. He had never been one to fuss much over food. He ate what he considered to be a healthy diet but, unlike his friends, he did not become enamoured of certain restaurants or insist on particular coffees or wines. Tonight, however, he was enjoying eating far more than usual. He could taste the freshness of the halibut and felt that with every bite he was taking in some of the strength and mystery of the sea.

They ate without talking; the man emitting slight noises of pleasure as he chewed. Halfway through their meal, Sarah arrived. She sat on the other side of the man with wavy hair, all three of them facing the window. David could not see her without leaning forward and turning his head. He tried to think of things with which to start a conversation and give him a reason to look at her, but he could think of nothing better than "it's a beautiful view," which he finally did say.

"Wait for it," the man responded. "I think we are in luck tonight."

Unlike the night before, it was a clear, cloudless evening. A golden path sparkled along the surface of the sea from the shore beneath them to where the sun touched the horizon. As they watched, the sun moved below the water, but the man beside him did not stop looking, and, when David leaned forward to pick up his glass of beer and use the opportunity to look sideways at Sarah, he saw that she was gazing as intently as the man was. Neither of them was looking at where the sun had been. Instead they were concentrating on a band of green sky between the darker blue of the beginning night and the lighter blue lingering on the horizon.

"There," the man said reverently.

David heard footsteps. The men in suits came and stood by their table, staring as well at the changing colour of the sky.

"There," the man quietly said again. "The colour of home."

Putting his glass back on the table, David stole another sideways glance. The four of them were so still, so absorbed. He felt as he had as a child when adults had been attentive to things he had not understood.

And then that short period of shifting light was over, and Sarah was standing, collecting plates, and the men in suits turned away, not back to their table, but out and down the hall.

Sarah did not return and the man beside him, who had been jovial and friendly earlier, now seemed as welcoming as a sleeping python.

After it was clear that Sarah would not return, and the man beside him was not going to break the silence, David stood, took his wallet out, and put a twenty dollar bill on the table.

This time, when he looked back before entering his car, he did not see the curtain of an upstairs window fall back into place as if someone had been watching him. The curtain was held to the side and she was standing there staring.

"What is that?" he asked, watching her roll the thin, gold coloured rod between her thumb and small fingers, her eyes closed, concentrating.

"An Ancil," she replied.

"What's it for?" he asked.

She didn't answer him, but continued to run it back and forth.

David did not know how long the storm had been going on. He woke to rain battering the sliding door, wind whistling around the corners of the cottage, and waves sounding too close and too large. As he lay there listening, he thought he heard another sound, a voice, coming closer, angry, possibly drunk. The wind and waves were so loud he was not sure if there was a voice, but then the glass door shattered as something heavy crashed on the floor and rolled across the room.

"I know you have it," the man yelled. "Who do you think I am? Did you think I would not know? Come out!"

David scrambled in the dark for his pants and shoes, not that he planned to go outside, but he did not want to meet this threat in his underwear, and he did not want to cut his feet on the shards of glass scattered on the floor.

He managed to slip on pants, but not find his shoes, before the man was there at the mouth of the broken door. David stayed still for a moment, crouched low, hoping to be hidden by shadow. A hand grabbed the back of his t-shirt and pulled him off balance. He fell and felt a sickening jab in his right knee; pain like he had never felt before tore up the inside of his thigh. The man yanked him through the door and dragged him towards the roaring sea. David twisted, trying to grip the ground with his feet. The man pulled him across a log and David fell over the side. His head snapped back, striking the ground, and then he was no longer aware of the rain, the wind, the man, or the glass embedded in his knee.

She came by their cottage just as they were finishing eating a dinner of sandwiches and potato chips. She knocked at the glass door, and his mother rose before he was able to, and invited her in. She saw the half-packed suitcases on the couch.

"You're leaving?" she asked.

"Yes," his mother answered.

"Tomorrow?"

"I'm afraid so."

She looked at David and he felt so guilty — even though there was nothing he could do — that it took all his resolve not to cry and not to turn away.

He put his plate in the sink and went with her outside.

"I'm sorry," he blurted out when they were away from the cottage.

He hadn't known how she had planned to make her own father stay, and his crying and shouting earlier had not had any impact on his mother's decision.

She did not address his apology but instead said, "I'll come tonight; listen for me." She made an O with her mouth and called out like an owl. "When you hear that, come outside. I'll be waiting."

He nodded, though he was not sure how easy that would be. Seeming to sense this, she knelt on the sand and pulled him down to face her.

"Please," she said, and for once she did not seem as strong and sure as she always had. "Will you?" She squeezed his hand. "I need your help."

He nodded. "If my mom wakes up, I'll run and meet you at the castle."

She laughed at this. Not making fun of him, he felt, but because he had surprised and impressed her. She hugged him then, and though he was too young and too small to fall in love, he did. And though he would not think of her when he was older and in the arms of other women, he would always compare those later embraces to this one and be unsatisfied.

That night he tried not to fall asleep. He lay on the couch, staring out the window, until he heard his mother's breathing deepen and small sighs come from where she lay on the bed around the corner of the open room. He woke to a hand shaking his shoulder and his friend standing over him; the finger at her lips barely visible in the dark. He followed her outside, slipping on the shoes he had left there, while she quietly slid the door shut behind them.

"I'm sorry I fell asleep," he whispered. "I'm sorry I didn't hear you call."

She smiled. "It's OK. It took longer than I thought it would."

He looked around and saw that the skyline was starting to glow with a new day.

She took his hand and they walked to the dragon log by which they had built their castle.

She sat down and patted the ground for him to join her.

"I need you to take something with you and hide it for me," she said.

"Will this help keep your father here?"

"He. We. Will be trapped here."

"Trapped?"

"Will you do it?"she asked.

"Yes."

"Lie down," she said.

When he had lain on his back she straddled his chest.

"Keep your eye open," she said.

She held the Ancil just above his left eye. She rolled her finger against her thumb, spinning the small gold rod. From its tip fell a single point of light.

At first all he felt was a slight irritation. He tried to blink, but the fingers of her other hand held his eyelids open.

His eye watered until he could no longer see her face and still his eye watered until it seemed like he was at the bottom of a pool. And there, on top of the pool, a star floated. As he watched, it sank down through the water of his eye, gracefully, slowly, determinedly.

It fell deeper than his vision could follow and he felt it inside, like the touch of the most beautiful note ever played. It moved into him and hid itself in a coral corner of his mind.

He lifted his head and heard his own voice moaning. Sarah was kneeling in front of him, a piece of blood covered glass in one hand, her other hand holding a towel to his knee which throbbed explosively. Behind her David saw the man who had fed him fish, who had dragged him from his cottage. The man was sitting on a chair, his nose bleeding. At his sides, holding an arm each, were the silent staring men in suits. Behind them David saw the shelves he had seen that morning, lined with carvings and gifts of the sea.

"How dare you?" the wavy haired man shouted, struggling. He was larger and stronger looking than the men holding him, but their hands pinioned his arms like vises and his efforts moved them not at all.

"And you," he said, turning to the man whose cottage this was, who held a shovel in his hand, looking quite prepared to use it, had probably used it already, judging by the wavy haired man's broken and bleeding nose. "You're part of this? I will rend you and your ripples. I will tear your threads out of existence. Your kin will never formulate again."

The man, who had looked so tender that morning, was calm and solid in the face of these threats.

"I aligned my threads with yours because you were of the best of us," he said. "But I will stay thick and large till my time is done before I ever let you return and impinge upon the others."

The man strained against his captors, yelling in frustration.

"Release me at once," he said to the men in suits, "and I will only reshape you."

But they did not.

The man noticed David was conscious and glared at him. David felt a small furtive movement somewhere behind his eyes.

"Father," Sarah said. "You can never return."

At this, the man's proud head fell to his chest and he wept loudly, louder than David had ever heard anyone cry. The room filled with his torment. David's skin could not keep it out. It was becoming his own and it was not something he was strong enough to bear.

"Please," the man said, looking at David. "If not me, let her go. It is not right that she no longer moves along the lines. That her grace does not enrich the others."

David found himself agreeing to this plea, but the carver was firm. "You know that can't be," he said.

David, who knew nothing of anything he had heard and only felt the anguish that penetrated him, called out "Why? Why can't it be?"

He looked at the woman who had been his friend when he was a boy and he, like then, was willing to do anything for her, even if it meant his life.

"My father and I are linked," she told him. "With me there, he could always find his way on our shared threads."

There was a flash of green light and before David was knocked backward by the man's body striking him, the room, and everything in it, the walls, the furniture and even those standing, seemed to him, just for a moment, to be like he had been told they were in science class at school, composed primarily of empty space. For just a moment, he could see through everything, as if nothing was in fact there and he was alone, adrift in the void between stars.

Then he was on the ground, the man behind him holding his neck in the crease of his elbow.

Sarah turned and calmly, as if the man's actions were of absolutely no concern, said simply "No."

And the man surprisingly released his grip.

David moved quickly away, turned back and saw the man nod at his daughter.

"I..." the man paused, taking a deep, long breath, "...will let you go."

The man reached out and squeezed his daughter's hand. "You must go. You must be part of home again." He softened his grip. "I'm sorry."

The sky showed the beginning traces of dawn, like it had that morning years before when she had given him the key — that was a grain of sand and also a star — to hold and hide, and take with him.

Gulls circled above as the grey sea crashed against the shore.

David's bare feet were cold; he leaned against the shovel in his hand, taking weight off his wounded knee. The others stood before him in shallow water, Sarah facing her father, her hands in his, he flanked by the silent men.

The man released his daughter's hands, looked at David, gave the slightest of nods to the carver of found wood, then turned, and with one hand in each of the suited men's, the three of them walked into the sea.

"Do you still have the Ancil?" she asked, after they had stared at the sea for a long time

"Of course," the carver said.

He reached into his pocket, pulled out the small golden rod and handed it to her.

She turned to David, took his hand, and led him up the beach.

He had not noticed, and had not thought to look for it, believing that it would have been long gone, but she led him to the log that had once had a head of a dragon. It was buried deeper, and the roots that had been teeth and horns were worn away.

There, behind the log, she sat atop him and held the rod's tip just above his open eye.

"Look," she said. "Look into the Ancil."

And, as when he was a child, she held the lids of his eye open until it watered freely. And moving up from its resting place in the folds of his mind, leaving a wake of childhood memories, a point of light pierced the bottom of his eye, rose up through his vision, floated for a moment on the surface of his world, then disappeared above his tears.

He held himself from asking if she must leave so soon. He knew that for her it was not soon at all and, as much as he wanted to, he would not ask her to linger. He did ask her one question. He was not sure she would be able to answer, but he knew if he didn't ask he would regret it for the rest of his life.

"Where are you from?"

She smiled.

"It's not really a where. Watch," she said.

She took a step back, then another and another, putting one foot behind her at a time. With each step she did not get any further away, but somehow, with each step, she became smaller and smaller, as if he were looking the wrong way through a telescope.

And then she was gone.

About the story

"Hold This Star For Me" started as an exploration of the idea of lost memory. My first draft began with a page and a half of the main character obsessed with the idea of repressed memory, feeling he'd had experiences in childhood he couldn't recall. After the story was finished, I realized this musing about the possibility of repressed memory had been my way into the story but the reader just needed the story, so I cut it all out.

I believe Stephen King in "On Writing" (though I've been scanning his book all morning and haven't found it) relates how Raymond Carver once knew he had a story though he only had the first sentence, something banal like: "She went to the closet and got out the vacuum cleaner." Carver didn't know what the story was about, only that it was there, and that following that first line would lead him to it.

"Hold This Star" was very much like this. I knew the protagonist was on a quest to uncover childhood memories but I had no idea what he was going to find. This makes "Hold This Star For Me" one of my personal favorites. Writing it was an act of discovery, and I was especially excited by how David uncovers two important strands of memories: contact with aliens and the very real human memories of his mother.

A question for the author

Q: When do you decide a story is finished?

A: I often don't know where a story is going, or how it will wrap up, until I get there. I believe that good stories are discoveries, or at least have an unpredictable organic quality, where the characters and events start to chart their own course. While some stories are thought out before I begin writing — or the end is known and it is the journey that needs to be discovered — I am often surprised by the ending and say to myself, "So that's what happens."

In terms of when I consider a story finished, as in, I've worked on it enough, not until it gets published. A most every time I reread a story, I find something I hadn't noticed before or that I could do better. Each time a story is rejected, I work on it before sending it out again. It is only that final stamp of approval that ends the process.

About the author

Mark David Adam lives on an island off the coast of British Columbia. When he is not foraging for edible and medicinal wild plants, playing funk guitar, or working at his day jobs, he writes short stories.

Hishi

David A. Gray

Hishi's claws ticked on the polished floor as she ran. The sound was barely audible, yet the teeming corridors emptied ahead of her. News had spread through the great city, out and down from the bloody throne room, that a new blend – an Excisor – had been dispatched to seek vengeance. Ten million people wondered who this Excisor was going to kill today. A very few knew, and prepared as best they could.

"Sure as The Scour hunts us all," the old ones whispered as she passed, pointing superstitiously up through the ceiling towards the roiling leaden cloud that blanketed the world. "The bonehawks will feast today."

The bonehawks feasted *every* day, Hishi's glanded memory stacks told her: Portmanteau's dead were rendered to remove every priceless, treacherous trace of metal, and the remains dropped through one of the mile-long vents in the bottom of the track as the gargantuan city rolled along its ancient course. Vast flocks of the vicious four-winged scavengers roosted on Portmanteau's underbelly, swooping down on Funereal days to try and catch the cascade of meat before it reached the steppe far below, there to be fought over by far more deadly competitors.

Hishi cut off the information flood with a thought. She had an Instruction from the Eternal him/herself, and would carry it out in perfectly and literally, as demanded. For the briefest of moments, the little Excisor wondered how things might be were she *not* to do so, and felt the gland at the top of her neck pulse. The surge of shame and contrition was so great that her step faltered and she came to a halt in an arching bloodwood cathedral, saw a flutter of red robes as a group of Spirituals scuttled to get out of her sight-line, never pausing in their endless repetition of the Histories.

"Deadliness and obedience," the Artificer who'd created Hishi had said paternally, not long after decanting. "You are my triumph. I took the best of the Assassin blend, added scar-cat senses and instincts, mixed in some peak-scaler, a touch of Human thinking, some Corrader-root contrariness, and a hundred other secret things. You are the epitome of single-minded loyalty. And," the leathery Agnost-root blender had muttered to himself, heedless of Hishi's keen hearing, "a thing of unsurpassed beauty and potential."

"Show us how lethal you are, how loyal," the masked, slumped figure on the throne had gasped, as Healing blend attendants had stanched the blood seeping through the priceless and ancient metal-ornamented robes. A wounded Courtier had handed The Eternal a long, thin bone pen, and a tiny scrap of parchment on a little tray made from priceless Original plastic. The nib had scratched steadily, ornately, and the Courtier had passed Hishi the completed Instruction. She had unfolded it, read it, carefully refolded the paper and placed it in a little pouch on her hip belt.

Hishi had bowed, turned and loped out of the blood-slicked throne room, as the healthy and walking wounded hurriedly cleared a path for her. She had glanced up once, through the grown crystal dome, past the mist-wreathed spires of this highest part of the city, at the Scour, where it roiled and seethed from horizon to horizon. Olders believed the turbulence moved with you as you walked, Hishi remembered. They believed it watched, and hungered. Hishi saw no such thing, but something deep in her gene memories made her relax a little more when she passed into the roofed corridors again.

Come to a halt in the vaulted church, Hishi replayed events so far, looking for unnoticed details that would aid her. "The past becomes the future," a bone-blade instructor had told her one day, as they'd sat nursing wounds. When Hishi had glared at him, he'd sighed and added: "A small omission one moment is your death the next."

She had not expected to be given an Instruction this day. She was barely out of the tank three months, summoned to an audience in the topmost levels of the city so the unquestioned ruler could give the seal of approval to his/her newest toy in front of fawning courtiers and cowed rivals. The new Artificer, whose blends were causing so much of a stir, had fussed round Hishi beforehand, measuring, assessing, murmuring: "You need to look your best, show them all!"

She had indeed shown them all her best: and her best was killing. No, *excising*. The difference was everything. Those who came before Hishi could *kill*. None could excise. She had showed them the difference.

"Assassins!" a towering gold-crested Courtier blend had shrieked as the group of hooded Maintainers had turned from their supposed duty repairing the floor of the coral floor, to pull stubby, fibrous, electromuscle thorn-throwers from their overalls. Thousands of tiny darts had sprayed the crystal-roofed room, cutting down Warriors alongside Clerks and Courtiers and a dozen more blends. They had killed. And the clumsy big Human-root Bodyguard blends had also killed, had swung bone swords with glacial speed, fired bulky living wood carbines, killed a hand of the attackers even as they were killed. They, and scores of glittering Courtiers, aloof foreign Ambassadors and liveried Servitors. But Hishi had *excised*.

The doomed Courtier had barely uttered the first syllable of its warning when Hishi's world had slowed. People became vectors and possibilities, estimates and presumptions. Thousands of glittering arcs marked the paths of the toxin-laden thorns in the air. Speedy attackers moved as through amber sap, hardened Soldiers lumbered, 1,000-generation-bred Bodyguards fought with steady predictable tedium.

Not Hishi. She'd moved through the slow-moving tableau, dodging deadly thorns, kicked out sideways at an attacker as she ran, seen a bouquet of rusty blood bloom from its neck, raised a long muscled tight-furred arm and sent a score of splinters of bone from her forearm, tiny vanes guiding them to throats, eyes, weak spots, delivering poisons brewed in her glands. A giant Bodyguard had screamed slowly as an assassin's stubby bone blade sliced through a gap in her overlapping chitin scale armor, had clubbed the smaller attacker down even as she fell.

Hishi saw everything, using eyes, ears, scent, bioelectric fields, vibration. She saw the dying attacker's finger squeeze the triggering bud on the pistol, heard 24 tiny darts as they sped out, calculated that five would pose a threat to The Eternal – who had moved not one hair's breadth since the warning scream – and had somersaulted over the stricken pair, taking a spread of darts to her back and shoulder. Her tightly packed layers of scar-cat fur and microfibers had stiffened and the darts had dug deep enough to hurt but not to deliver the poison on their pulsing tips.

Hishi had plotted a course towards the perfectly motionless figure on the throne. But not directly to it. She had discounted obvious threat and tactical considerations, leaving simple defensive reaction to the slow Guards. Hishi's route across the throne room was designed to take her from one attacker to another, to remove them in the simplest, most economical manner possible, then move on to the next. She'd jumped, sliced through an assassin's hood with a claw, felt warm blood that triggered the tiny poison cells in the needle-like tips to dispense targeted toxins. She'd sidestepped a knotted Reaver commander swinging a long diamond-edged blade like a scythe, trying to hold a clot of attackers back even as tiny darts sprang from his face and arms. A frantic Courtier, loyalty coming to the fore where martial skills were lacking, had grappled with a hooded assassin, taking multiple deep slashes to her arms and face. Hishi could have paused, saved her, but that would have cost her an early interception with another attacker who was more likely to reach The Eternal, so she had left the brave servant to die, then had struck her targeted attacker so hard she'd felt its chest cavity collapse, had ripped her hand on its shattered spinebone.

Another had stabbed at Hishi with a long glass blade. She'd taken the strike along her ribs in order to avoid losing momentum, nipped the off-balance attacker with a poison spur on her heel, spun onward. *This* was excising, she had thought triumphantly, danced on, slashed, leaped, kicked, eviscerated.

Suddenly, disappointingly, it had all been over.

Time had sped up again.

A score of attackers had lain dead, and twice as many court officials and guests. The last assassin, laid open from neck to waist by Hishi's retractable claws, had lain bleeding, inches from the edge of The Eternal's robe.

Hishi had felt her ruler's shrouded eyes on her, smelled an unfamiliar musk under a camouflaging perfume, knew she was being studied by a great many senses. She scented blood, too, saw a thin bone handle protruding from the Eternal's chest, heard the slow glutinous trickle of fluids onto the old metal-inset fabric. Hishi felt her gland pulse, thought she would die from shame and guilt. She hadn't seen the knife in play, should have seen it, tracked it. She had gasped in near physical pain at her failure.

The mask had nodded infinitesimally, then a bloodied Soldier had wrenched the dying attacker back, exposed the face, and a chorus of hisses had come from those nearest. It was no Assassin blend, but a hard-edged, scale-skinned rangy blend like none Hishi had seen before. An Ambusher, her glands whispered, and Hishi remembered. The Ambusher blend had been a step too far, at least in Portmanteau and its client cities. They had proven useful in the endless skirmishes with the nomads the city encountered on its long loop through the lowland plains, but conventional wisdom had it that they had been given a little too much native DNA and not enough Original, and they were … unsettling to be around. *Unsettling,* Hishi thought. I know how that feels. Then the notion evaporated.

The Ambushers had all but vanished, employed now only by some of the more traditional sub-clans in Portmanteau.

This one suddenly stiffened and thrashed in a way it shouldn't have from Hishi's precision strike alone, its double-jointed sinewy limbs hitting the smooth floor so hard she heard them fracture. A suicide trigger, then. Much like her own, only hers was keyed to the displeasure of The Eternal. That last seemed unfair, Hishi thought, but the thought was snatched away before she could even consider it.

A spindly Reader was hurried forwards as Guards held the dying Ambusher down. Long fingers clasped the leathery skull. A moment later, the Ambusher lay still, and the Reader knelt and whispered something to The Eternal Courtier, who in turn leaned close to the wounded ruler and spoke. That was when The Eternal had actually spoken directly to Hishi, reproachfully telling her to prove her lethality. And she'd been handed the Instruction.

"The sponsor for this is Matriarch Eventide," the paper had read. "Excise all responsible."

Hishi, in the gloom of the cathedral, spotted an osmosis port set in the dark wooden wall. She was close to the edge of safe palace territory, and so touched her wrist to the little iris. She was recognized, and a moment later, a warm rush of nutrients and chemicals flowed into her veins, and a torrent of information into her glands and head. Some information seemed extraneous, some vital. She saw her route, already selected to take her through the most public of thoroughfares, the grandest of plazas. She frowned for a moment at the showiness and inefficiency of this, then obedience kicked in. All the new information would take a minute to permeate, infuse and be sorted, so she slowed her triple hearts and let her mind wander. She saw her reflection in the lustrous oiled wood, studied it critically. Small, by most standards, maybe half the height of a towering Soldier blend. A touch feline, she knew, if you took the tight-coiled scar-cat as your base assumption of feline appearance. The genes had been incorporated into previous blends, she remembered, but never with much success, as their implacable and frankly cruel instincts were too ingrained. A true memory, then: the Artificer studying Hishi fresh from the tank and muttering to himself. "Of all the creatures they made and left, of all the monsters and sports and tricks, the scar-cat was the most beautiful and least wise," he'd whispered to no-one. "And you, my dear, *you* are the first to do it justice."

Hishi had some of the scar-cat in her impenetrable dun fur, fast-twitch muscles, and ability to track multiple moving objects. And, for a reason that she knew to be vanity on the part of her maker, a fold to her ears that served no purpose save to mark her as a pet, a project. Hishi understood why she was what she was: a perfect instrument, designed for a role. But something about the knowledge that she had been molded for the esthetic pleasures of another, *that* was wrong. She felt a cold fury rise up at that, then other, saner, Original traits kicked in and reined the scar-cat heritage back, choked it. She saw in the dark mirror the first of a new blend, small, taut, gender-less. An angry thought emerged, was muffled as treacherous.

The tiny osmosis port closed, bringing Hishi back to the moment. Now, it was time to excise. She sped out of the cathedral, heard the Spirituals chanting, wondered if she would be included in their spoken histories of the city.

Two tiers below, Hishi passed out of the palace. The change was not noticeable to the casual eye, not even marked officially. But from here, though the orders of The Eternal were still sacrosanct, his/her will still law, she was in the city proper. And from this point on she would be mingling with teeming millions who cared less for their ruler than themselves, or their own clan leaders. She felt danger, opportunity and freedom. Hishi felt alive.

This close to the royal chambers and receptions, the corridors were wide and clean, decorated with rich coral mosaic and fringed with rare plants. House Eternal Courtiers huddled, watched by Guards, but not so closely they couldn't conduct sensitive business with other city functionaries and visiting envoys. Hishi saw it all with her eyes, knew it all from an endless well of stored and inherited memories. She had only to wonder, and she knew. Knew too much, she suspected, blinking it to a halt so she could focus on the real, the present. And in that moment, she cursed internally. Ahead, a fork in the thoroughfare, the corridor to the left was still emptying, while the one to the right was crowded with people looking her way. Her designated route was to the left.

In the rarefied, scandal-filled tiers of the palace, especially following an assassination attempt on The Eternal, that was only to be expected. There were whispers, coded hand signals, pheromones, and a hundred other ways of passing information fast and unnoticed. But here, she should have been free to travel without anyone knowing. To perform her function. Instead, Hishi realized, she was *expected*. And that could only be intentional. A signal, and an entertainment for the colossal city this day. Hishi felt warring priorities: should she take the route given, presumably by the royal court, knowing it would be slower and offer less chance of success? Or should she Excise with the single-minded goal of fulfilling The Eternal's Instruction? Hishi decided instantly: Excision was everything. She concentrated, pulled a complete map of Portmanteau from her glands, knew every inch of the thousands of miles of corridors, halls, shafts, drains, and highways.

Hishi ran the expected way for a short time, savoring the bubble of solitude that surrounded her, planning. At a narrow intersection of three corridors, she took the one that led up, and back into the palace proper, passing a pair of surprised Soldiers at rest, not pausing, but knowing they would raise some kind of alarm at her change of course.

The challenge was to leave the palace not just unseen, but with some clever misdirection. She sprinted through a small park roofed in cellulose, herds of wandering plants tracking her and instinctively moving in tandem, to the irritation of masked Gardener blends who were trying to trim tiny hard iridescent scales from their crowns.

Down, then, and to a slim grown bone arch whose span narrowed to at its arched peak. At this end, a hulking Guard, standing immobile in chitin plated armor, a serrated coral blade longer than Hishi resting point-first on the floor. At the other, the start of a route that pointed straight to the heart of the distant Caltrop tower.

Hishi could have run past, ducked, but she needed to make a statement, and so feigned a dodge and then, as the Guard lunged, she struck down with one claw, slicing between arm plates as the brute extended its reach. A tiny drop of paralyzing agent, hardly noticed, but staggering the Guard enough that Hishi had plenty of time to strike again, delivering another dose to a momentarily exposed neck. Then to the back of one leg.

Again, and the Guard slumped, unconscious. But not for long.

Hishi leaped over the prone figure, ran, and halfway across, dropped off the edge of the unrailed arch, falling a tier to a ledge whose filigreed coral window overlooked a wide spiral stair that led down through the bowels of the city. She glimpsed, saw, heard, felt a dozen Secretaries there, conducting business. The ledge was narrow, crumbling, windblown. Hishi waited, unseen, patient.

This high up she had a clear view between two colossal towers, out across rooftops, out to the planet's surface, the near-flat horizon. The memories formed.

Scour. They'd named the planet after the terror that blanketed it, those unwilling Originals. The spoken litanies preserved by the very Spirituals who chanted without pause somewhere behind Hishi said that the ships had crashed here, eaten and dissolved by the living clouds even as they landed. Everything metal, plastic, contrived, from the ships' hulls to the tiny living machines in many of the Originals' bodies, had been consumed, the remains abraded to bone dust by the swirling storm.

The few survivors, from the 20 remembered old species, had fled, shorn of every tool and device they relied on. There, in the vast plains, dodging the Scour storms that stooped from the sky and dug mile-wide scars from horizon to horizon, they met lethally designed flora and fauna. Vast herds of fast-moving plants with toxins in every leaf, ferocious armored herbivores, flitting razor-beaked flying things and tireless predators on, below, and through the churned soil. All of them living around, dodging, following after, and screaming defiance at the storms. All deadly to the naked arrivals.

Hishi saw a Scour storm moving parallel to the giant city, seemingly blind to its existence, digging a ragged deep trench as it spun, moving, the city whispered to her, away. Fifty miles out, a pair of storms danced around each other, all the while moving in loops towards the northern sea. Hishi's eyes zoomed in, enhancing every detail.

A swarm of jagged little threshers let the wind pull them along in the backwash of the storm, where they tore chunks from creatures dazed from its passing. Preying on them, sucking the jagged omnivores up in wide grinding jaws, a group of reinworms. One of the 40-foot serpents was thrashing up a cloud of ichor and grit as a flock of trepaner birds swooped and plunged hollow sucking lances through its bulbous head. On the outskirts, rippers and spined seers, tearing at stragglers and each other, and following them all, a wide carpet of swaying ambulatory plants, elegant and three times as tall as Hishi, with a spread of pink motile light-gathering fronds on top, and a tangle of dragging roots festooned with paralysis-causing barbed hooks.

The deep wound in the ground would soon be smoothed by rain and wind, dappled with ponds, filled with fast-growing moss and opportunistic wind-blown prey and predators alike. All looking for food, and the tiny – and ever decreasing – amounts of metal left in the soil. The Originals, Hishi recalled, had not just relied on metal and artificial materials, they had contained it in abundance flowing through their blood, rich and versatile. The Scour had devoured them, replenished itself.

Hishi wondered about those memories. How could things so flimsy, so ill-suited to live, have survived here? She felt her Human and other Original genes, enjoyed their cunning and reasoning, but doubted the grandiose stories attributed to those beings, doubted even that there *was* anything above the Scour. How could there be?

The Secretaries moved on, a chattering gaggle. Hishi swung through the window, pushing the coral panel ahead, catching it before it fell, turning and placing it back where it had rested. She ran on, down, unrecognized.

While plugged into the osmosis port, she'd tasked her glands with sending new resources to the tiny distilleries in her hands, feet, glands and elbows, and already she felt hundreds of tiny lethal bone spikes sliding into queued muscle-fired channels powered by one-shot electro cells. Her retractable claws had added layers of extra ceramic to their outer edges, and the little toxin-bulbs around their bases were full. Hishi was not by personality or design prone to boasting, but she felt a certain pride in her abilities, and recognized that she was the pinnacle of the 1,000 generations of gene-tweaking that had followed the discovery of the first Cache. Well, she corrected, not the pinnacle: a pinnacle. It was just that some pinnacles were more fit to the task than others. A gland memory quickly interjected the cautionary tale of the recent Revenant blend attempted in House Astrogator's secondary city. All accounts pointed to that reckless House's attempts at a radical mix of Scholar, Hr'esche root, and the murderous Hook birds, plus some of the still-incompletely-understood strands from the Cache. The Astrogator Emperator had announced that a catastrophic failure in one of Dunedin's axles had caused the small city to stall in the path of a Scour, but a handful of survivors plucked from the grit by House Hood Scavengers told a very different story, of sabotage by panicked Scientificers to try and eliminate the uncontrollable blend before it could take flight.

Hishi paused on the stair. No alarms, no footfalls that spoke of anything out of the ordinary, no wafting pheromone orders. She was free to carry out her duty.

Matriarch Eventide, then, of House Caltrop. Memories bloomed, and Hishi ran on. The old Matriarch would not submit to the Instruction, and Caltrop was a formidable clan. An assassination attempt, while not unheard-of in inner and inter-House politics, was significant, more so in that every House, faction, sub-clan and nomad group would be watching closely to see how The Eternal reacted. On Scour, hesitation meant weakness meant death. The Eternal could have sent a small army rampaging through Portmanteau, but that would have shown a lack of confidence, and over-reacting was another perceived sign of weakness. Also, damaging a city's living structure was unacceptable. Hishi liked that her purpose was to make necessary things happen tidily.

She raced through rooms and chambers, across living stone, warm wood, engineered coral and cellulose, never slowing. She ran with no mind to misdirection; she simply took the fastest way down from the high tiers and inwards to the geographical center of the palace city. Word of her route would spread by mouth, bird, and chem-signal through the palace's sap conduits. But the eventual target would be secret until there were no other possible options. And Hishi had a complex series of bluffs, turns, and evasions prepared.

The ornate tiers slowly gave way to more utilitarian corridors whose dead wood and stone walls dated them to before the pre-Cache explosion in organic building artifice. She slipped unnoticed through halls busy with shift change Administers, the multi-strand and root support cadres that kept House Eternal's gargantuan palace city and its 23 subsidiary and client cities running smoothly. Hishi had been tanked with a complete if simplistic knowledge of the great Houses' affairs, and knew that the cities' survival depended upon a vastly complex system of manufacturing, cultivation, gathering and trading with friend and foe alike. At any given time, a capital city like Portmanteau would have scores of thousands of outriders – Herders, Merchants, Reavers, and Sifters and many more specialties – coming and going via hoists, scoops, drags and the giant access decks found on every hundredth core-stone Track tower.

She passed through the throngs like a wraith, stepping between the heartbeats, dancing through fleeting spaces. To Hishi it felt like an easy run through virtually motionless statues. To the bustling crowds of Administers, slow and deliberate of thought and action, it was as if an outside door had been left ajar and a tiny dusty vortex was whirling through their midst, brushing them no harder than a feather.

Some tiers beneath that, she cut through a broad wet chamber full of moonflowers, their waving pale stalks turning to follow the never-seen satellites claimed to be somewhere above The Scour. Cold, muted, blue light came from a million hair-wide pinprick optic veins that twisted and coiled into thick cables and finally emerged on a flat sky-facing terrace somewhere on the city's skin. Hundreds of Botanicals in white woven coveralls bustled around in the soaking soil, tapping minuscule quantities of metal-rich sap from the root bulbs. They paid Hishi no mind as she raced along narrow raised boards crisscrossing the fields: like many specialties, every successive generation was tending towards more focus on their role, and less interest in society as a whole. Hishi had only a brief sliver of actual life experience to fall back on, but her gene memory told her that the tens of thousands of Botanicals had seldom set foot outside the lower mid-cavern levels these past few generations.

Hishi came to a cargo capillary, where stooped, burly simian/Scour-dragon-stock Workers were racking big seed-pod-shaped containers in front of a bio-valve that opened with a wet suck every few beats, then closed, sending the container down to the bowels of the city. She raised a hand, and the senior Worker dutifully trotted over, his eyes darting up and down Hishi, agitated, unsure but respectful. *Good,* Hishi thought. *I'm faster than word of my description.*

"Duty of The Eternal," she said simply, and the sinewy Worker picked the most reasonable course of action.

"We are honored," he said. "If you can delay by only enough heartbeats to allow this current load to descend, I can clear a pod for you. These are only for kindling seeds, and are volatile from seepage..."

Hishi sniffed, detected a faint, acrid scent, that triggered a new memory. Kindling seeds were collected by nomads and those cities whose tracks arched above the ember forest belt, or passed close by. The flammable, sticky liquid inside the seeds was a volatile and valuable trade commodity, especially when the great cities were in conjunction, and war loomed. And, Hishi knew, Portmanteau was about to converge with House Recurve. Recurve was arguably as powerful as House Eternal, and the last time their vast capital cities had passed at a distance of 40 miles, 100 years ago, casualties on both sides had been high. Very high. Rumor had it that that some facing towers had yet to regrow their full height, but Hishi considered that detail nothing more than an instructional tale for fresh tanklings.

The next convergence of the elevated tracks was this very month. And this time the channels would pass so close that the cities' extremities would be within a hairsbreadth of each other – a ridiculously close 100 paces – for weeks. Yet another puzzle for Historians to study: some Tracks circled the world alone, others intersected and looped close to others, a few even circled on a huge closed perfect circle at one pole. In one place, a Track climbed above another, even, and then there was the Yard, where hundreds of the soaring stone channels met, meshed and joined. The Yard was where the course of a city might change, for the good of the ancient structure, and sometimes the ill of its inhabitants.

Portmanteau's course took it close to other cities quite regularly. Most of those were now clients and satellites. But not Recurve. And few came as close as that behemoth. At such range, a war could reduce them both to three-mile-high ruins, thus the daily exchange of Envoys. But The Eternal was no fool, and House Eternal had not risen to the top of the heap through complacence. As diplomats rode out, so vast trade caravans kept pace below the city, delivering mountains of wartime supplies. The kindling seeds – alongside other nasty chemicals and surprises – were hoisted up to hidden arbalests and throwers, alongside great wound bows and grappling arms. Thousands of Warriors would wait, too, by drawbridges and hoists. The thought thrilled Hishi, and repelled her.

She snapped back to focus, cursing the unasked-for memories for distracting her, when an Assassin might have come on her unprepared. No, never unprepared. But marginally less prepared. And Hishi needed to succeed. The Worker was gesturing to an empty pod, and Hishi got in with a nod. He looked relieved that she was going.

The organic shell sealed with a snick, and a few moments later the translucent casing was dropped into the rhythmically contracting tube. Down, ever down.

Threshold was not for the claustrophobic. Here, the ancient, indestructible core-rock base of the city melded with the less enduring materials added over the eons. The Originals, wandering their murderous new world, had found some of the slow-moving structures to be no more than colossal platforms on slow-turning wheels. Others were motionless, stripped by The Scour after some accident or decision had caused them to stall. Still more had been on the move in various stages of completion.

In Portmanteau's rare case, the city was apparently abandoned near-finished and intact, with living ironwood binding precision-cut stone blocks to form a mile-high fortress, complete with pinprick lights, power, irrigation systems, and still-living protein vats. More vitally, as with all the still-moving cities, enough of the billions of nutrient-fed bio-muscle pistons were functional enough to move turn the core-rock gears and drive shafts that kept the colossus moving.

The survivors, those few who the litanies said lived through the Wandering Time, had scaled a Track tower and moved in. Wary, depleted and grateful, they had vowed never to abandon their new haven.

The structure was now almost four times the initial height and double the width, a dazzling layered puzzle of wood, stone, bone, cell-glass, and coral, and a hundred combinations thereof. Hishi felt pride in the Original City, as such a trait, along with a tightly-linked loyalty to The Eternal, had been deemed useful.

And so as she brushed the last pod fibers from her fur and strode away from the sliced-open container on its landing pad, she was suitably impressed by the mile-wide chamber whose roof arched many hundreds of paces above gigantic stone and wood supporting pillars. Threshold was where the city met, people said. Incoming cargo and trade/war goods and parties were lifted in through massive portals, vast mountains of food and consumables came up and down for packing and distribution, and giant grown parts for the wheels and axles were hauled to access pits in the stone floor. Add to that innumerable shops, stalls, dens, pleasurariums and bio-pits, and teeming crowds, and you had Threshold in all its exciting, seedy, dangerous, opportunistic glory.

Hishi immediately liked it, in the way her scar-cat DNA liked the promise of a dusk hunt. She set off at an easy lope, aware that eyes might already be on her. Hishi took in a thousand scents, hundreds of distinct blends of what were once just those 20 Original races. Giant muscled Porters hauled bales of harvested pelt as big as Dust-Ox, tiny darting Messengers dashed past with secrets, Reavers strutted in long-legged packs, Artificers stood lost in calculation, Ambassadors moved arrogantly like plains-galleons, and visitors gawped at it all. Woven through this tapestry, assassins stalked, spies peered, plotters schemed, and poisoners waited.

Now, Hishi needed to be creative and fast. She knew Caltrop would be waiting: even if they were not aware of the discovery of their guilt, Mistress Eventide would have her people prepared. But if they even relaxed a little, that tipped the odds a fraction. Her presence here in Threshold was no secret, but her destination would still be a matter of debate.

The first attack came in open view of thousands of eager witnesses. A trio of dusty Nomads carrying heavy saddlebags were passing close by Hishi in the throng, when, as one, they shrugged off the bulging leather sacks and lunged at her, short glass blades in each hand. Hishi had no warning, but plenty of time to study her limited options. Nomads were a catch-all name for a whole subset of blends. All of which were designed for harsh conditions outside the cities. These were typical of the type: lean, fast and, Hishi realized as a dodged blade abruptly reversed course and slashed a shallow score across her ribs, double jointed. And, another surprise, possessed of accelerated reactions. That last, as a slash that should have raked out the close-set eyes of the lead attacker, only nicked the wide snout. Hishi had been taken by surprise, and felt humiliation and rage rise up. Her blood roared, glands surged and reduced the world slowed to a crawl, flooded her body with her own, vastly superior accelerants, and Hishi waited, motionless. The Nomads hesitated at that, exchanged the briefest, most fatal of puzzled glances, that allowed Hishi a space between heartbeats. She kicked out, felt tough exoskeleton snap under her heel, fired a brace of targeted darts from her backward-flung balancing arm. Nomads' genes were hardwired to fear toxins, Hishi knew, through hundreds of generations of encounters with the worst that the planet could devise. So even though their rough hides and inbuilt immunity should have had them ignore the darts, they flinched back, attack arcs forgotten. And died gurgling as Hishi turned and leaped, claws bare.

The gathering crowd, well aware of who Hishi was by now, stamped in a thunderous approval. Not necessarily for The Eternal, she understood, but for the raw display. Something in Hishi responded, and an impulse rose, was followed. She bent to slash the nearest satchel, spilling out hundreds of glass beads, the heart of every one holding a tiny grain of reddish metal. Taking a double handful, Hishi threw them in the air, a glittering fountain. The scene turned into a mad scramble, and Hishi ran, unseen for the most part.

Hishi gazed at the three prone guards. Regrettable and messy, as they would be missed, and that would eliminate the element of surprise. But they'd blundered onto the scene when they were meant to be elsewhere. That was troubling. As was her very use of poison so early in her mission: Guards were a hard blend to render unconscious, and she'd been rushed into using a powerful and lethal toxin. They'd dropped the moment she'd raked all three across their vulnerable eye-slits on one motion.

Hishi had been careful, passing under Caltrop's massive turret and heading for the fringes of sub-clan Flint territory. Even when she'd backtracked up the outside of a wind-scarred stone escarpment, she'd angled as if to sneak into the Stirrup embassy, only swinging across a half-mile-deep chasm at the last moment to steal through a narrow window into her real target. She was sure she'd not been tracked. And yet ... she had been met at every step, fought, forced to Excise.

No matter. She raced on, up a wide spiral staircase with indentations worn into the stone treads. Ahead, heavy footfalls coming down, a trace of musky sweat containing glanded accelerators: vulpine-blended Caltrop Warriors. Hishi flooded her body with the boosters she would need, snicked long curved claws from their sheaths and squeezed a range of toxins along tiny veins. She flicked a long arm and a hundred tiny guided seed slivers flew out, the native hunting plant-gene twist giving them a heat-seeking hunger. Time slowed, Hishi sped up.

Hishi looked down, a clear mile drop to the Track. She'd never been outside on the facing edge of the city before, never seen the Track through her own eyes, to form real memories. She had to wait out here for long enough that the Caltrop retainers would take the planted clues and assume she'd retreated after the barrack-room battle, to lick her wounds, and would set off in presumed pursuit to finish her. Hishi did need a moment, she admitted, for rents to knit, toxins to flush. She had excised 267 living things thus far, and it was becoming messy, brutal, not beautiful. She'd climbed out of a window, edged up the slick living rock wall and on to a tiny ledge, where she now clung, unseen, battered by the cold wind. Vertigo was not an issue, or fear: Hishi's poise here no different than had she required to walk in a straight line through a genteel garden level. Only the outcome should she make a mistake would differ.

She looked down, ahead. Restorers were visible on the Track, making sure even tiny scrapes and gouges in the mile-wide core-stone channel were smoothed over, clearing any worrisome debris thrown onto the U-shaped canyon. Down in the raw deep wound off to the side were crews of Sifters, alert for any particles of metal not consumed by The Scour, but mostly seeking another Cache. There had only been two such stores found, Hishi knew, in many thousands of years; fragments of whatever civilization had created the great moving cities, then vanished. Each Cache had contained enough specialized knowledge to give the unwilling colonists previously unimaginable advances in genetics and bio technology.

Much further off, Hishi's predator-spliced eyes could see a Scour moving slowly anti-spinward: churning up the Bone Wastes again. Somewhere in that vast dead expanse sat the shell of the great city the stunned first arrivals had named Necropolis. Hishi had tasted memories of recent travelers who'd seen the colossus, tilted and ruined at the shattered end of a Track, smoothed a little more by every passing Scour it could no longer outrun. Perhaps I can see that for myself some day, she thought, then unwillingly discarded the idea as counterproductive.

When finally she calculated it was safe to drop down and in again, Hishi was stiff with the cold, but alert, and driven by the need to move, to obey the Instruction. The wrecked room had been cleared of the bodies, but not the slick of blood, or the smell. She padded along the edge, and took a small door that led to an unassuming staircase.

Hishi's focus was all on fighting, moving up. Her movements were more spare, to conserve energy and to allow a dozen gashes to heal. Her working memory contracted to snippets. Dropping from a vaulted ceiling onto the helmets of five surprised warriors, claws flashing. Slicing through a toughened cell-glass wall with de-bonding enzymes, through a tanking ward, cutting down a clan Warrior as she raised a razor-edged ceramic blade. A leap across a chasm, claws scrabbling for purchase, a swing into a waste shaft a spliced second before a Guard looked down. A tumbling, chaotic battle with a kilted, gnarled Forager, retired to court duty but still fast as a grit snake and too thick skinned for toxins, requiring a choke hold to make him gasp for air and allow a single drop of deadly oil to be forced in his mouth.

A cold pond room with a dozen lithe junior nobles of Aristocratic blend, a flurry of billowing scarp-scorpion silk robes and thrown crown thorns, falling like leaves in the Scour to Hishi's leaping slashes and strikes. A long bloody score along her back, fast clotted and knitted. 502 excised. Killed, something in her head whispered, and was muffled.

No more stairs. This was the top of Caltrop territory. Hishi stepped over the body of a proud Bodyguard blend, almost sorry to have spattered that fine feathered crest with blood. At the same time, scornful that effort had been wasted on decoration, rather than efficiency. She strode through an old-fashioned grand observatory, the centerpiece of which was a dented, priceless alloy head-sized encased in amber, dead, useless. An Artificed Intelligence, she recalled, supposedly brought by the Originals, wrenched from one of the dissolving starships, the Caltrop, after it smashed on the great plain. Inside the sphere were useless fragments of carbon-cell brain. In as much as Hishi had any interest in ancient history, she wondered at the hopeless naivety of the stranded survivors, to preserve that, when they had had exactly no chance of ever leaving this world.

A rush of near-silent feet, the silken rustle of an Assassin's strangling ropes and thin coated blades. Hishi ached, slowed time, and let the scar-cat loose.

"You are the new Excisor blend, I assume?"

Hishi nodded.

The old Human-root woman pursed pale lips, looked Hishi up and down. "Too much," she said disapprovingly. "Before you do what you must, let us talk?"

Hishi felt no need to talk, but a small, subversive part of her wanted to listen. Eventide was old, near ancient, in fact, as close to an Original as had existed since the Caches were discovered. She had seen many generations come and go, must have traversed this world a hundred times over. Hishi sought completion, but also a *reason*, so she could best understand why she was here, dappled in the blood of hundreds of citizens. Her warring instincts found a truce in common sense: she would use the brief pause to flush some toxins from her blood, saturate her lungs with more air, isolate and eject a hundred slivers and ceramic fragments that had penetrated her body. Her toxin buds were dry, her thorn chambers empty, three claws snapped off, and she ached all over. An ear was ragged, too, which oddly irked Hishi more than the more serious injuries.

She heard a slow regular drip, noticed her own blood falling slowly to the bespattered coral floor. Five Ambushers lay dead around the old wooden chair, alongside a half dozen retainers who'd tried to impede her; a towering Humanelve Counsellor lay bubbling in her own blood. A dozen others poised to make a desperate rush. A fruitless rush. Maybe. She sensed every inch of the modest circular turret room, heard treads thundering up the single staircase, saw the locked hatch to the roof, felt a tiny movement of air through minuscule gaps in the big round window that overlooked the rooftops.

Hishi nodded, noting the beads of sweat on the withered clan ruler's wrinkled face. Eventide was easily over 1,000 years old, one of the early beneficiaries of Cache-given advances that had slowed aging in those few ruling-class specialties deemed fit for the laborious and painful process of re-gening an adult. She was as pure a strain as Hishi had heard of, one of the relative ancients who'd come from basic alterations to make the feeble colonists tough enough to survive. Human look and build, aquatic scales for durability, largish cranium for intelligence, a scattering of strands from winged omnivores for speed and focus, Hishi thought. Definitely live birthed, too.

"Who are you?"

"I am an Excisor," Hishi said, puzzled.

The ancient one scowled impatiently. "No, who are you? I hear you have a name."

"Hishi," she said simply.

"And you chose this name? Or was it that twisted Artificer who made you?"

"I chose."

"Yet you have no siblings, no family, you are also, unless my senses fail me, obedience-bound and genderless. Why do you need a name?"

Hishi felt that sting, though she did not know why. "I will not always be genderless; only for the duration of my service," she said, parroting the words the Artificer had use to her, no, *about* her, to Courtiers and Scientificers. "For clarity of focus and purpose, no distractions. When my service is done, I will choose to be 'she'."

A look of pity crossed Eventide's face. "We've come to this," she said softly. "Sending our children to kill for us. So," Eventide said more gruffly, "that fool of a boy on the throne sent you to try and dispose of me. I knew he would, eventually. The weak ones always do. Did he say why?"

The Eternal was male? And young? Neither had even occurred to Hishi before.

Which struck her as odd, also. Curiosity, she had, but not a full range of it. That bothered her, and then it didn't. She almost killed the old woman there and then, loyalty and outrage lifting a hand to strike. But she held back, waiting for an admission of guilt that would end her task cleanly. Also, she was curious.

"Because you tried to kill hi…. The Eternal," Hishi said. "I was Instructed to Excise all responsible."

"Before you do your horrid duty, let me show you something," the old matriarch said in a dry whisper. Hishi paused, clawed hand raised, time crippled to a crawl. Another drip of her own blood slowed in its passage to the bespattered coral floor.

The old lady fished carefully about her plain tunic, keeping lightly scaled hands where Hishi could see them, Hishi noted approvingly. Then Eventide held out a folded scrap of parchment. Hishi didn't take her eyes off the woman, but took the paper between two claws and flicked it open. She glanced at it, fast. The familiar script read: "Assassinate person of Eternal. 7/10 Turn, this day."

Hishi was confused, and in the dissected second her attention was elsewhere, the Matriarch lashed out with surprising speed, a hardened hand striking Hishi in the throat. The blow would have crushed her windpipe had the Excisor not thrown herself backwards as it landed, skidding across the blood-soaked coral-glass floor, gasping for air. The Matriarch's Guards leaped forward to complete the kill, but Hishi used the slick floor's lack of traction and slithered a body-length clear, vaulting to her feet to slash down on a mailed fist where the hand armor and forearm plates met, near-severing the appendage. A thrown bone blade penetrated Hishi's tough layered fur at the shoulder, the point protruding out the back. Her glands shunted the pain away, closed off redundant arteries and in a smooth motion, Hishi gripped the blade in a hand and wrenched it out, continuing the sweep to send it through the eye-slit of the second Guard. She jumped backwards, a flip, landing in front of the defiant Matriarch, and lifted her good hand to strike.

The old woman's face showed no fear. "The Instruction was real, lass. Do with that knowledge what you will."

Hishi struck, tearing the woman's throat open, using the last drops of every toxin she had to ensure no revival was possible. She turned, letting the light old body fall, and saw a wave of furious retainers and Gaurds rushing toward her. Without a thought, Hishi jumped back and through stained-amber window behind the Matriarch's chair. A spray of darts and projectiles caught her as she tumbled, one ripping into the back of her head.

Hishi saw a bottomless chasm, and tried to right herself for a controlled fall. She struck a stone parapet, felt something break, then knew nothing more.

Fascinating, Hishi thought through a haze of pain so great that it almost was surreal enough to be able to pretend it was happening to someone else. Even while unconscious I tracked my own position. I did not know I could do that. She was lying on her back, so could see a tracery of glowing lines stretching up though blackness, like the webs rot-spiders drifted on ahead of a Scour storm. She tried to examine the data and immediately passed out. When she came to again, she was thinking a little more logically and directed her glands to numb the pain and give her stimulants. This was, to Hishi's surprise, only partly effective. Tasks that would have taken a thought, were now beyond her.

She listened, unable to see a thing. Other senses, then. A low hum and constant slight vibration. A very slight breeze on the side of her face. She tried to move, couldn't, and a rare panic took hold. Am I paralyzed? She howled, then, and felt the fur on her back tear out in clumps as she came free of the ground with a sticky ripping sound.

When Hishi came to again, still in pitch black, she moved carefully, found she had some control over limited gland function, and boosted her senses to ultra violet and thermal spectrums, with an active ping added. So, she was lying on core-stone, a curving platform fully 50 paces long that sloped down to left and right. Only a thick accumulation of sticky oil-saturated grit had prevented her from sliding off. Behind Hishi the core-stone wall was moving, smoothly and ceaselessly. Not just moving. Rotating. Hishi could sense heat from a small gap around the semicircular ledge she sat on. Not semicircular, she reasoned. Circular. And huge.

A distant part of her mind finally made sense of the data from her fall, matching course with maps. She'd descended a full, incredible, two miles and some. That she had survived at all was down to the ancient design of Caltrop's fortress: the outer walls were grown and built to be too smooth for interlopers – internal or some of the more enterprising external predators – and like Portmanteau itself, widened as they descended. A full third of Hishi's drop had been down a sloped section of city wall, then the architectural tricks to funnel wind and rain had played in her favor, treating the tiny, broken Excisor like a piece of storm-blown trash, funneling her down and away efficiently.

Hish had bounced from outcrops, slid down a vast fungus-choked air shaft, tumbled across a slope of Dayshade vines, ripped through a wide bio pipe and sluiced down an overflow drain on the resultant nutrient torrent. Ever downward, light and limp, bouncing. And breaking, healing, breaking again, partially healing again as she fell.

And now, Hishi realized with a shock, she was on one of the giant wheel hubs down in Axle. The undercity, off-limits to civilized people. The moving wall was a wheel, stretching up and away, and down to the Track. A few paces to either side and ... Hishi shuddered. Wait: fear? Shock? These emotions should not have been available to an Excisor. She remembered a blow to the back of her head, ceramic slivers from Guards' weapons slicing into her, and reached up with shaky hands. Instead of tight muscle and fur, a jagged sticky mess. She had some glanded abilities, still, but clearly there was serious damage. Also, surprisingly, clear thinking, no, not clear, just not limited. Hishi experimented, imagined The Eternal dying, felt a rush of agony so great she knew she would die too, were it true. So, the suicide gland was still there. But she knew, now, that her crushing loyalty was artificial, glanded, enforced, as was the idiotic idea of her life ending just because The Eternal's did. The fool boy's, she corrected, remembering Eventide's words. Hishi healed fast, knew for sure that she would have a very brief time in which to act to keep her new-found clear-headedness. If she wanted to. Dared to.

Hishi decided, called up the stored plans of her own body and then, looked deep into the schematics for the complex and remarkable gland cluster. Dozens, scores of tiny individual glands and manufactories, all working together. But some wrecked now, and some a hindrance. Hishi took a deep ragged breath, not allowing her conscious mind to catch up, snicked out an undamaged razor-sharp claw and struck deep at the base of her skull. She screamed, then, and dug with brutal precision until the pain stole away her consciousness once more.

Hishi dragged herself up another rung. 3,086. She'd told herself she could climb no more of the narrow stone notches on the dangling stalactite ladder, at 2,000. And at 3,000 had thought she might throw herself backwards, off, down to the wheel again, this time to bounce and die. But she had an Instruction to finish. And the clarity to know how.

3,203: no more rungs. A lichen-covered corridor of wet core-stone, shuffling Axle inhabitants from no specialties Hishi recognized, and some her glanded memories had told her were long-since eradicated. Hands helping her, too weak to fight back, a nutrient tap, a cup. Blackness again.

Hishi came to slowly, tried to spring to her feet, managed only to roll over and vomit on herself in the dark. Her night vision flared too bright, showing a rough-hewn chamber with indistinct figures around her. Then it snapped off and the blackness was total, only to be replaced by an overlap of thermal map and motion vectors from the slow draught of warm stale air. She tried to shake her head, screamed in agony.

Strong hands gripped her head and a cup was held to her bruised lips.

"Don't fight, lass," a grating, slow voice urged. "Someone made a proper mess of the back of your head, near tore that abomination of a manufactory cluster out your head."

"Me," Hishi tried to say, "suicide gland. Take it out." It came out as a whisper but whoever was holding the cup, seemed to understand.

"Thought as much. Well, we don't have The Eternal's Medicants here, lass, but we've some experience in removing the worst of the new tortures. Drink: this will hurt less if you do."

Hishi didn't drink, and as more hands held her, the pain in her head multiplied a thousand-fold. She thrashed and howled but forbade her thorns to fire or her claws to extrude. And in time she passed out.

"How long can they survive?" Hishi and the stooped old Healer called Chirur sat on the edge of Portmanteau's blunt frontal slab, directly above the leading edge of one of the mountainous wheels. Its fellows stretched to both sides, across the width of the stone canyon of the Track. The noise – millions of tons of stone rolling over stone – was less brutal than Hishi had expected, due, Chirur had told her, to the incredible smoothness of the wheels and Track, even after these uncounted centuries. It vibrated every part of you, Hishi thought, reducing you to nothing. A stiff but pleasant wind blew in their faces, dispelling, for a moment, the ever-present Axle levels smell of grease and waste.

She didn't have access to her gland memories any more: that pulsing black organ had been buried in an organic settling bed, Chirur said, to have it do some good at last.

"Why not just kill them?" she asked, as a group of figures far below and a little ahead were prodded off a wooden hoist onto the smooth stone track bottom.

"Where would be the lesson in that?" Chirur replied. "This way, anyone who cares to see The Eternal's mercy for his opponents need only look down."

Most of the 20 or so people were trotting away from the trundling mass of the city, slowly increasing the gap between themselves and the grinding wheels. A few were running towards the distant edges, and the cliffs rising there on both sides. A few simply sat down in the path of the relentless wheels.

"Can they escape?"

"The only escape is under the wheels, or if they're still alive when we go over a vent and they fancy a drop all the way down to the monsters that shadow Portmanteau looking for scraps. And once in a while a hookbill will take one to lay its eggs in."

Hishi shuddered. "How long?"

"How long can they walk without stopping? There are tales of victims – the fleeter, hardier blends – lasting five-days, 100-days, even more."

Hishi perked up. The old exiled healer was fond of telling stories, and in the ten day since Hishi had arrived near death in Axle, he had proven a kind companion. And a vital one in the dark, unmapped, dangerous base levels of the city. Here, Hishi had learned, the detritus, the unwanted, the unsuitable, ended up. Both inorganic and organic. Discontinued blends, fugitives from Eternal justice, illegal immigrants to the city, and more. And, raining down on them, the byproducts of the capital city. Axle was where waste was processed, the endless gears and muscle engines located, the proceeds of illicit deals hidden, swapped, traded, along with lives.

"More?" she prodded gently.

"There are tales of lights, campfires glimpsed way ahead on the long straight sections of the Track, the flames carefully shielded from those gazing down from above, but sometimes visible from way down at our level. People say there are entire tribes living on the Track, who've perfected scavenging from the things that blow, fall, and are trapped in the Track."

"Do you believe those tales?"

The old man smiled: "I believe a lot of things that are not true."

Hishi leaned forward to see one of the people below as the vast turn of the wheel lost them to sight. She'd been shy of going too close to the mountainous stone rollers at first, haunted by a fragmented memory of waking, broken, on the curving axle. Now, she was confident, happy to hang over the drop by a hand to satisfy her curiosity.

Portmanteau trundled ceaselessly on dozens of rows of the polished stone cylinders, each row made up of 20 wide smooth solid wheels, separated from their fellows by a hand's breadth.

Chirur hissed in concern and she smiled inwardly. Once the gland was removed and a ready supply of clean, if illicit nutrients had come her way, Hishi had healed fast. But not totally. She'd lost the tip of an ear, which now delighted her for the anguish it would have caused the Artificer, and had pale scars all over her body. She was close to her old speed and balance, though lacking some of the powerful aids the gland had given her. But though she was free of the compulsion to please, to die for, The Eternal, Hishi was still driven by duty.

"I need to go back," she said bluntly.

Chirur was silent, and instead of answering, nodded out to the right into the foothills. "Recurve coming," he said conversationally, as if discussing the weather. "Convergence in a three-day. Be busy upstairs, with all those Strategists and Soldiers and Diplomats running around."

Hishi nodded. She zoomed in on the distant curve of another elevated Track as it looped round through the plain to run parallel to Portmanteau's course, traced way back to a distant smudge on the horizon.

Chirur continued: "Not so many people know, the traffic that goes back and forth down these levels come a convergence. From the high and mighty doing secret deals, to people looking to start a new life..."

Hishi felt something new, something not hostile. The thought wasn't banished, but neither did she know what to do with it. She touched the old healer softly on the shoulder with a furred hand, and padded away.

The stir was audible when Hishi limped in through the giant double doors of the High Reception. The room was truly grand, a billion shards of Scour-glass covering every span of wall, floor, and vaulted ceiling. Behind the high throne, a stained-crystal coral fan, colored and dyed to show a scene from the story of the Landing, Originals stumbling from a ruined warship even as The Scour's tiny living machines ate it.

The Eternal was surrounded at a respectful distance by whip-smart Strategist blends, and a score of military specialties. At the back, the stooped Artificer who'd made her, and whose name she realized she had never heard. Watching her, expressionless.

The atmosphere was tense but not panicked. And Hishi knew from her lope up through the city that war was, thus far, at arm's length.

The Eternal's Secretary let the babble of voices rise, then snapped a long tendril and there was silence. Hishi knew her appearance broke a score of Court protocols. Bruised and scarred. More deeply than they knew.

She padded forwards, stopping three paces from the throne, noting the Guards, three from before, one new.

The Eternal's ornate mask was fixed on her. The Secretary coughed, and spoke: "The Eternal wishes it to be known that we are pleased to see our loyal instrument returned alive ..."

"They knew I was coming. It was a test," Hishi said simply. She stared at the mask. There was an outraged pause, then the Secretary started to puff up to deliver a rebuke. A gloved hand was raised, silencing the courtier. It leaned close to The Eternal, and something passed between them. The courtier straightened and spoke: "Why do you say that?"

Hishi took a breath: this close, The Eternal's presence was almost overpowering. Her conclusions came in a rush: "Because The Eternal didn't move. Not a twitch. Not even to avoid harm. And because I would have seen the blade. And the blood, it smelled ... wrong. Old. Not real."

Everything stilled, quieted. Hishi could sense Bodyguards tense, Diplomats watch with feverish interest. She hadn't mentioned Eventide's note, sensed that The Eternal was waiting to find out if she knew. Hishi said nothing and there was a barely perceptible feeling of tension ebbing. The Eternal nodded to the Secretary, and something was whispered.

The Secretary stood tall, spoke loud and clear to the whole room: "A test of loyalty of a new blend, yes, and a lesson at the same time. Matriarch Eventide had questioned our rule, sowed dissent. An example had to be made, that just one loyal servant could excise even the most powerful sub-clan. The completion of the Instruction means..."

"Not completion," Hishi said quietly, and there was a scandalized hush. She sensed a Guard move, a Human-root female.

" 'All responsible' not Excised," Hishi said. "Instruction wording very specific."

She sensed The Eternal stir, felt the tissue around the empty suicide gland bud twitch, a knot of scar tissue in her head acknowledge the repeated signal, but no more happened. The Guard hesitated. The Eternal's mask trembled. Time slowed down.

About the story

"Hishi" came from a bunch of directions at once. I was worrying about my daughter and the world I'm raising her in, where rich old white men seem intent on burning it all down and ensuring she has no rights. And where we as a species seem to be sending our kics to war, or to bomb and kill. So I had in mind a character who had all her life ahead, all her potential, but was choked by the actions of these old men. But who would triumph, in the end. Kind of. The world — Scour — was inspired a little by those old stories where we know society is the ruins of an older civilization, a tiny bit by railway tracks (a minor obsession), and a lot by a wish to take an extreme situation and imagine how we'd be after 10,000 years of forced evolution. The things we would do if we had to, then because we could. Also, I'm an avid student of Ottoman history, and of the Crusades, and Europe's Hundred Years War. Imagine, for a moment Constantinople on wheels.

"Hishi" was — and is — a standalone story, but in the process of editing, I realized this is her first chapter as a person in a strange world. I know where she goes next, even if I don't ever write it.

A question for the author

Q: From where you do you draw inspiration for your characters?"

A: I take something from myself at a young age. when I used to stagger home from the library with armfuls of peculiar/comforting-smelling classic sci-fi, full of anticipation and alert for the local crazed bullies. But it's from my kids that I take most, now: that heady mix of potential, hope, happiness and occasional heartbreak. If any of my characters convey even a little of that sense of opportunity amidst the darkness, then I'm flattered and happy.

About the author

Gray is an exiled Scots creative director and journalist living in NYC. He works for a range of print and digital magazines and brands, and every night he climbs to the roof of his Brooklyn apartment building and squints at the Manhattan skyline, wondering how it might look in a century or few. Sometimes he thinks it will be a glittering gem, other times, a flooded ruin. Or maybe a bit of both.

Copyright

Metaphorosis Publishing

Metaphorosis offers beautifully written science fiction and fantasy. Our projects include:

Metaphorosis Magazine

Metaphorosis, a weekly magazine of SFF short stories, including stories from all the authors in this anthology. Find out more at magazine.metaphorosis.com, and sign up to be notified of new stories.

Metaphorosis Books

Recent books from Metaphorosis can be found at <u>books.metaphorosis.com</u>, and include:

Metaphorosis 2017

Metaphorosis 2016

All the stories from *Metaphorosis* magazine's second year.

Almost all the stories from *Metaphorosis* magazine's first year.

Metaphorosis: Best of 2017

The best science fiction and fantasy stories from *Metaphorosis'* 2nd year.

Metaphorosis: Best of 2016

The best science fiction and fantasy stories from *Metaphorosis'* 1st year.

Reading 5X5

Five stories, five times

Twenty-five SFF authors, five base stories, five versions of each – see how different writers take on the same material.

Reading 5X5

Writers' Edition

All the stories from the regular, readers' edition, plus two extra stories, the story seed, and authors' notes.

Best Vegan SFF of 2017

The best vegan science fiction and fantasy stories of 2017!

Best Vegan SFF of 2016

The best vegan science fiction and fantasy stories of 2016!

Susurrus

A darkly romantic story of magic, love, and suffering.